I0710155

A Day Trip to Brighton

The Mysteries of Stickleback Hollow®

By C.S. Woolley

A Mightier Than the Sword UK Publication

©2023

A Day Trip to Brighton

The Mysteries of Stickleback Hollow®

By C. S. Woolley

A Mightier Than the Sword UK Publication

Paperback Edition

ISBN Paperback 978-1-7385919-5-4

ISBN Hardback 978-1-7385919-6-1

ISBN Kindle 978-1-7385919-4-7

Cover Design by Get Covers

For

Jen

Author's Note

Thanks for taking the time to read *A Day Trip to Brighton*, I hope you like the book. For those of you who are just diving into the series, the year is 1840 and though our title heroine has been living in England for several years, this is her first trip to the seaside resort of Brighton.

The seaside towns of Britain are as varied and wonderful as the people that comprise the countries of the United Kingdom of Great Britain and Northern Ireland. I spent many happy university weekends on the beach near Scarborough and Whitby. Blackpool was a frequent stop for the fun of the seaside coupled with the beauty and wonder of the illuminations. Cornwall and Devon provided opportunities for holidays with friends (and some camping nightmares) with cliff scaling, surfing, and chasing the tide at night - during a neep tide (some of us gave up, some of us may have kept going until the sea was eventually located, and some of us may have stayed in the house and enjoyed the wonders of large measures of Baileys).

Though in all of my adventures and beach holidays in the UK, I never had quite the same experience as Lady Sarah. The worst thing I have seen washed up on the beach is a string of dead jellyfish from the Irish Sea.

But in writing this book, I enjoyed flashing back to the memories of my homeland, the happy memories with family and friends, and the improvisation of using a rather uniquely patterned rug for a twister board when we had exhausted all movie options.

Though I do have many treasured memories associated with the seaside, this book does deal with human trafficking and the poor treatment of other human beings in the name of prostitution. If you have concerns about modern human trafficking, the effects on your community, and wish to take a stand against it, I urge you to get in contact with your nearest coalition against Human Trafficking to support the work they do and bring an end to this modern day slavery.

I hope that you enjoy this book as it is one that I enjoyed writing, and will treasure for all the joy it has reminded me of.

Kia Kaha.

The Characters

Lady Sarah Montgomery Baird Watson-Wentworth

The heroine

Brigadier George Webb-Kneelingroach

Lord of Grangeback and Lady Sarah's Guardian

Bosworth

The butler

Mrs Bosworth

The housekeeper

Cooky

The cook

Mr Alexander Hunter

A huntsman and groundskeeper of Grangeback

Pattinson

An Akita, Alexander's hunting dog

Constable Arwyn Evans

Policeman in Stickleback Hollow

Doctor Jack Hales

The doctor in Stickleback Hollow

Miss Angela Baker

Seamstress and mother of the Baker boys

Stanley Baker

Son of Miss Baker

Lee Baker

Son of Miss Baker

Reverend Percy Butterfield

The vicar in Stickleback Hollow

Mr Thomas Egerton

Son of Wilbraham & Elizabeth

Mr Edward Christopher Egerton

Son of Wilbraham & Elizabeth

Mr Richard Hales

Son of Doctor Hales

Mr Oliver Henry Brown

An American Gentleman, Cousin to the Egerton Family

Sylvia

Lady Sarah's Companion and Lady's Maid.

Lady Szonja, Countess of Huntingdon

Cousin of the Egertons, Ally of Lady Sarah

Captain Jonnes Smith

Chief Constable of the Cheshire Police Force

Constable Thompson Buckley

A constable of Stickleback Hollow

Chapter 1

Heavy is the heart that is torn between two men, and Lady Sarah Montgomery Baird Watson-Wentworth was no exception. She had spent many sleepless nights considering the two men that had both proposed to her.

On the one hand, she had Mr Oliver Henry Brown, an American, but a charming American. He was the cousin of the Egertons of Tatton Park, and had recently taken up residence in the neighbourhood at Duffleton Hall. There was a great deal of talk amongst the locals of the villages and surrounding hamlets, that Duffleton Hall was a cursed place. Of the former owners, Mr Oliver Cartwright had left Stickleback Hollow on the business of the crown and been so badly tortured by the Chinese authorities he was too sick to ever return home; and Mr Daniel Cooper had been found murdered in the hall.

Duffleton had stood empty for sometime, but then was taken over by a psychopathic doctor who had been experimenting on, then murdering women he considered to be fallen after kidnapping them from the hospital.

Yet, none of this had stopped Mr Brown from buying the house and moving in.

On the other hand, there was Mr Alexander Hunter, the illegitimate son of Lady Sarah's guardian, who had not only been recognised by his father but named as co-heir of the estate with Lady Sarah.

She had been in love with him from the moment she had laid eyes on him, but their romance had been beset by kidnappings, machinations of others, grief and sheer stupidity.

Mr Hunter and her ladyship had been engaged before, during which Lady Sarah had become pregnant and lost their child. A event that had sent Mr Hunter spiralling into depression that caused him to abandon his fiancée and his home to battle with his own demons.

Though she still loved him, Lady Sarah did not know if she could trust him not to hurt and abandon her again.

She had been back and forth between the two men so many times, and every time she felt she had made a decision, she found so reason to change her mind again.

Sylvia, her lady's maid and companion, had listened

to every possible choice with good humour and far more grace than she had ever displayed with anyone else. She knew that the decision was a hard one for her mistress to make, and her patience was due, in part, to the fact that whoever she chose to accept would be a permanent part of Sylvia's life as well.

"Perhaps there is a third choice, one who has not yet presented himself," Sylvia suggested during yet another long debate about the merits of the two men.

"I do not think that a third suitor would improve this situation," Lady Sarah sighed as she slumped back on the sofa in her private rooms.

"No?" Sylvia asked with an air of mischief.

"What are you thinking of?" Lady Sarah frowned at her friend, mystified by her attitude.

"During our time at Chillington Hall, Richard Hales spent a great deal of time in your company. Am I mistaken in my logic that he would make a very suitable husband?" Sylvia asked, doing her best to suppress a smile.

"Richard is a friend, a good friend, who has never shown any romantic interest in me. I would not encourage him to join this circus of emotion," Lady Sarah replied with a heavy sigh.

"I understand, but you will have to make a choice soon," Sylvia warned her.

"I am all too aware of that fact. Perhaps there is another way to approach this," her ladyship said and shook her head.

"One man shall be hurt, and one shall rejoice. There is no way to avoid that. But for all that you are torturing yourself about a right decision, your heart already knows who you should marry. Until you are ready to listen to your heart and set aside your head, you will be stuck in this place," Sylvia said flatly.

Lady Sarah did not reply, she knew that Sylvia was right, but that did not mean she liked hearing what her companion had to say.

Brigadier George Webb-Kneelingroach was sat in his study. The room was his safe retreat from the stresses of his estate and the problems of love-sick children.

But it was also the place where he and his son could

sit and talk in an open and honest manner that could not be done in any other part of the manor.

"Do you think she will accept my proposal?" Mr Alexander Hunter was sat opposite his father, in one of two high-backed, leather chairs, and the pair of them were nursing glasses of whisky as they spoke.

"That I cannot say. The workings of the female mind are as much of a mystery to me as they are to you," the brigadier sighed and shook his head. "But I can say that I hope she will accept you. It will certainly make your shared inheritance much simpler."

Mr Hunter could not help but laugh at his father's poor attempt at a joke.

"I wonder if there is anything that can be done to convince her that I am the better, and correct, choice," Alex mused.

"Perhaps there is. Romance is something that women value," the brigadier said with a slight shrug.

"What if we were to go away for a few days, the whole household," Mr Hunter said suddenly.

"And to where might we go?" the brigadier asked with interest.

"What if we were to away to Brighton?" Mr Hunter asked with a small measure of excitement. "Lady Sarah has never been to the seaside before, at least not in England. It would be a new experience for her, and there are the sunsets over the vast ocean that will provide the romance," Alex continued.

"What a capital idea! We must tell the ladies at once. I must summon Mrs Bosworth to oversee the packing, but there is much to be done. I must send a telegram to arrange for a hotel on such short notice," George cried as he leapt to his feet and rang the bell to summon Mrs Bosworth.

"And perhaps we do not inform our neighbours of our intention," Mr Hunter said with a slight smile curling at the corner of his mouth.

"Perhaps you are right. Though we could extend the invitation to the doctor and Richard Hales to join us, the brigadier suggested.

"Then yourself and Sylvia will have companions to talk with,," Mr Hunter grinned as the door was opened by Mrs Bosworth.

"Mrs Bosworth, we are to away to Brighton. Send an invitation to Doctor Hales and his son to join us, and begin packing right away. The Baker Boys, Sylvia, Lady Sarah and myself shall all be going, as well as Mr Hunter and our invitees. We shall also be in need of Cooky and Bosworth," the brigadier announced with a broad smile.

"And perhaps somewhere to stay?" Mrs Bosworth asked with a raised eyebrow.

"Yes, yes, details are yours to arrange," the brigadier said with good humour.

"Very good," Mrs Bosworth said dryly and left the room.

"One day you will find she is gone and have no idea what you are going to do with yourself," Mr Hunter warned his father.

"One day I will not wake, and you will be the one who has to replace her," George replied with a grin, and all Mr Hunter could do was shake his head.

Chapter 2

octor Jack Hales sat in his living room reading the newspaper. His feet were up and resting on a plush footstool. A fire burned in then hearth and there were no patients in need of attention, there were no great mysteries or emergencies that required his attention. He had received a letter the day before from his son, Gordon, who had eloped to America.

The news from across the Atlantic had been good, and it had given the doctor a lot of peace to know that his son was thriving in his new life away from the shores of his birth.

His other son, Richard, had been packing for his return to university for the past two days, though he had been staying with his father for some time now, so long that the college had sent several letters demanding his return or that he official take a sabbatical from his studies.

Richard had been a much needed rock of stability for the doctor during a turbulent time, but he had a future to forge on his own and he could not stay in Stickleback Hollow forever.

But Richard was not ready to leave. He had been dragging his feet on his packing as his mind was a whirl with ideas and a need to remain in the village.

He had finally made a decision about what he should be doing, and went in search of his father to inform him of his decision.

"Father, I will not be returning to university this year. I have decided to take a sabbatical until the next year. I am not ready to return to my studies, and I did not want to leave you after such a disruptive time," Richard announced as he found his father in the sitting room.

"I see, and what will you do with your time?" the doctor asked as he lowered his paper and folded it in half before throwing it into his lap

"I wish to work with you, assist you in your practice here in the village. When you retire, I want to take over here in Stickleback Hollow as the new doctor, and learning about my future patients early, can only help," Richard replied.

The doctor sat and considered his son's proposal carefully before he made a response.

"Very well, but you shall have no special favours

because I am your father. You are not yet a doctor, so you will not see any patients alone and will not override my diagnoses in public. If you disagree with me, then we shall disagree in private. Is that understood?" Jack asked his son as he put down his paper, and got to his feet.

"It is, father," Richard said without any reservation.

"Then very well, my assistant you shall be," the doctor held out his hand to his son to shake on the agreement, and Richard grasped his hand with enthusiasm.

"Write to your college, and we shall begin at once," the doctor said happily.

Constable Arwyn Evans awoke to a morning he had dreaded for several weeks. Captain Jonnes Smith, the Chief Constable of the Cheshire Police Constabulary, had visited to inform Arwyn that a new constable would be arriving in Stickleback Hollow to help with the village policing.

It was not that Arwyn was adverse to having some help in the village. It was not just the village that he covered but the surrounding hamlets and manor houses as well, and help covering such an area was something that the constable could not deny would make his life easier. But it was the fact that the previous new constable, Owens, had turned out to behind a series of kidnappings and killings that had led to Lady Sarah's miscarriage, as well as the destruction of several other lives.

The bitter taste left by the previous constable meant that Arwyn was nervous about any new policeman coming to the village. He often had support from other constables based in Chester, but it took hours for them to reach the village, and it was becoming more and more inconvenient to wait for assistance in certain situations.

So when he awoke the morning that the new constable was due to arrive, it took every bit of self-control Arwyn possessed to not roll over and go straight back to sleep.

He closed his eyes briefly, but forced himself back awake, and swung his legs over the edge of the bed. He got up and staggered to the basin to wash his face and dress before he trudged down the stairs to cook his breakfast.

He had lived alone in the police house for several years now, and he had grown quite used to the quiet and peace that came with being able to shut out the rest of the world at the end of the day.

Sharing the house with another, with who, he would also have to work with day in, day out, was not a prospect that he relished.

He cooked his breakfast and ate in silence. He tidied the kitchen and then went to make sure that the bed in the second room had been made up.

Miss Angela Baker had offered to help make the place ready for the new arrival, and had done a wonderful job cleaning and preparing the second bedroom, as well as taking off years of grime and dust in the kitchen.

Arwyn had wondered why Miss Baker had offered to help, and realised that though she was in demand for her seamstress skills, since her sons had begun an apprenticeship with Lady Sarah, she was lonely.

The constable had taken to calling on her every day at 5pm to share a pot of tea and a chat about their respective days. Sometimes it became dinner afterwards as well, other times they were interrupted by a village emergency or someone else coming to call on Miss Baker. But it had become part of his routine, and as he stood, looking at the neat and tidy second bedroom, he wondered how much was about to change in the village.

At 8 o'clock in the morning, the new constable arrived. The chief constable had sent him along with only the trap driver for company. He brought with him three large bags and a steamer trunk that looked like it had been dragged all over the world.

"Good morning," Arwyn greeted his new arrival with the small amount of enthusiasm he could muster.

"Good morning, Constable Thompson Buckley," the fresh-faced young man said with excitement as he leapt down from the trap and offered his hand to Arwyn.

Constable Evans looked at it for a moment, on the verge of declining his hand until he knew the youth better, but he pushed aside his concerns and opted instead to briefly shake it.

"Pleased to meet you," was all that Arwyn could manage to say.

"I am excited about being here. Rumour is that this is a cursed position. I heard a lot about the man before me from the other policemen in Chester, but I promise you, I am not going to be like him!" Thompson said earnestly.

"Less cursed and more a position that needs a certain

personality to endure," Arwyn allowed but said no more on the subject.

The two men worked together to get the bags and the steamer trunk off the trap, and sent the driver on his way back to the city. It took around an hour for the new constable to unpack and settle into his room. Arwyn then gave him a tour of the police house before setting out to show him the village.

Thompson was not surprised by the welcome he received, or by the way that Arwyn was pulled aside by almost every villager for a quiet word in his ear. By the time they reached the manor, the good humour he had felt about being assigned to the village had all but evaporated.

"They're a mistrusting bunch," Constable Buckley shook his head as they walked up the long drive to Grangeback Manor.

"No, they are merely cautious after the problems we have had in the past. I would not judge them too harshly on it," Arwyn shrugged.

"But they are assuming that I will be like the others," Thompson complained.

Not only had Thompson learned more of the details of

exactly what had happened with Constable Owens, he was learning about Constable Cartwright as well, and the bad taste that both men had left in the mouths of the Stickleback Hollow residents.

"Then show them that you are different, earn their trust, and give them back some faith in others," Arwyn said with irritation grinding his words. He had not time for whining, no time for unfairness. He was a Welshman and as such, was automatically seen as less than his English counterparts. He had earned everything he had worked for, especially the trust and respect of the people he served in the village.

They finally reached the manor door and knocked three times before Bosworth appeared to answer it.

"My apologies, constable, we are somewhat engaged in packing activities," the butler said as he welcomed the two men into the hall.

"Another trip? Where to this time?" Arwyn couldn't help but laugh slightly.

"To Brighton. Cooky and I are to go as well, so should you need anything in our absence, Mrs Bosworth will be here," the butler said as he showed the two men to the conservatory at the rear of the west wing.

It was a room that Arwyn had never been in, not in all his years in Stickleback Hollow or all his visits to the manor. It was filled with tropical plants and seemed to be exceptionally hot. There were a few chairs made from wicker situated amongst the foliage, but from what the two constables could see, it was purely a place for the plants.

"Miss Sylvia, Constable Evans and Constable Buckley are here," Bosworth announced and the lady's maid rose from seemingly nowhere with a look of fury on her face.

She marched over to where the two policemen stood and without hesitation, slapped Thompson Buckley hard across the face.

Chapter 3

The violent outburst caught both the butler and Constable Evans off guard, but it was clear from Constable Buckley's response that he would not have expected anything else from her.

"Lovely to see you again too, Sylvia," he said as he rubbed his cheek.

"How dare you set foot in this house!" she bellowed and her rage caused her eyes to widen.

"I shall fetch her ladyship," Bosworth said with alarm and disappeared off, moving much faster than Arwyn had ever thought the man capable of.

"Do you know who this man is? What he did?" Sylvia demanded of Arwyn.

"I have had very little time to discover anything about him," Constable Evans stammered, shocked to see Sylvia so enraged.

"I am sorry about what happened, Sylvia, truly," Thompson protested. It looked as though Sylvia would strike the man again but as she raised her hand, Bosworth returned with Lady Sarah.

"Sylvia!" Lady Sarah exclaimed and the companion held back her blow.

"My apologies, my lady," Sylvia said, her cheeks flushed and her fists balled in anger.

"Please, tell me, what has you so enraged?" Lady Sarah asked gently, her voice full of concern.

"This, this, man! He is the reason that I was left with nothing!" Sylvia cried.

"I see. Sir, before you became a policeman, were you employed in a household as a footman?" Lady Sarah asked.

"I was," Thompson replied.

"And you told your employer that Sylvia was with child," Lady Sarah said.

"I did," Constable Buckley answered with shame.

"Was it your child?" Constable Evans asked.

"No, but that hardly matters. I caused a great deal of harm in my overzealous attitude. I should not have said anything to our former employers. It was not my place to speak out. I was angry and felt wronged. But whatever the reason, I cost you your home and livelihood. I am sorry. I know that there is nothing I can do now to redeem myself, but when I realised how much damage I had done, I made a decision to leave and do better with my life. It is what led me to becoming the man I am now," the constable said earnestly.

"Then we shall say no more about it, and this incident will be forgotten for the moment," Lady Sarah said and looked at both Constable Buckley and Sylvia for their agreement. The pair nodded their heads and Bosworth escorted Sylvia from the conservatory to rest in her room and calm herself.

"My apologies, Lady Sarah, we came as part of showing Constable Buckley they village. I had no idea that he and Sylvia shared such a history," Constable Evans apologised.

"So this is our newest village resident?" Lady Sarah asked with surprise.

"I am, my lady, Constable Thompson Buckley, at your service," he bowed to Lady Sarah which caused Arwyn to groan inwardly, and Lady Sarah to suppress her amusement.

"And you have met with the rest of the village?" Lady Sarah enquired, her voice betraying a slight laugh as she spoke.

"I have. It has been most educational. My predecessors have made my position a difficult one," Constable Buckley said.

"We all face the same pressures when filling a new role. Whoever held it before us leaves a legacy. Sometimes it is one we have to overcome to redeem the role, other times it is a shadow cast that means we must reinvent our role to make it our own so that we are not continually compared unfavourably to what has come before. Remember that you are your own man, and you can forge whatever path you choose. But do not blame the expectations of others for your own fears and failings, you are the one who ultimately chooses what to allow to affect you," Lady Sarah replied wisely and watched a look of utter confusion wash over the new constable.

"We've taken enough of your time today, your ladyship," Constable Evans jumped in before Thompson could respond to her advice.

"We shall see you when we return from Brighton. It was nice to meet you, constable," Lady Sarah said and watched Arwyn steer Thompson out of the room without another word.

It was barely twenty minutes since the constables had left the manor when another visitor arrived to call upon the household.

Miss Beaumont and Mr Claydon arrived in high spirits. Sylvia was resting in her room, worrying that Thompson Buckley's appearance in the village would ruin her life a second time.

Mr Hunter had returned to the lodge to pack his belongings for the trip to Brighton. Mrs Bosworth was occupied with arrangements, and Cooky was barking orders in the kitchen, accompanied by a barking Pattinson, and the three beagle puppies that had been a gift to Sylvia and the Baker boys from Charlotte Giffard.

Brigadier was sat in his study and Lady Sarah had moved from the conservatory to the library, where Bosworth announced the two guests.

"Good day, Lady Sarah, we come bearing invitations," Mr Claydon said in his booming voice, his excitement and delight evident as he rocked back and forth on the balls of his feet.

"How wonderful, does this mean you have set a date for your marriage?" Lady Sarah asked with anticipation.

"We have, but I would like to speak to the brigadier, if I may," Mr Claydon replied.

"Of course, Bosworth, would you be so kind to take Mr Claydon to the study to speak with the brigadier. Then arrange for tea to be brought for Miss Beaumont and I," Lady Sarah asked.

"Of course, your ladyship," Bosworth replied and led Mr Claydon from the room.

The two women remained in the library and talked about flowers and dresses. But flowers and dresses were the last thing on Mr Claydon's mind.

Bosworth knocked on the door of the study and announced him. The brigadier was sat behind his desk looking through piles of papers.

"Ah, Mitchell, capital to see you, is there something urgent you wished to discuss?" George asked in a distracted manner.

"Not urgent, but it is important," Mitchell Claydon said as he sat down in one of the vacant chairs opposite the desk.

"I see, well, by all means, what can I help you with?" the brigadier asked as he set his papers aside and leant forward to rest his elbows on his desk.

"I wished to ask for your permission to hold our wedding feast on the lower paddock by the church. We are happy to pay you for the time we spend on your land and we will ensure that it is cleared of all rubbish before the end of the festivities," Mitchell said with baited breath.

"My dear fellow, of course you can! In fact, I will have Cooky prepare the feast, the footmen will serve it, and I will not hear of taking a fee for the use of the land. I believe we still have the canvas tent that we erected for the last spring festival," George said with a wide smile.

"My friend, that is all too generous, you must let me compensate you," Mitchell argued but the brigadier held up his hands.

"No, I will not hear of it. Consider it my gift to you and your beautiful bride. You do not need any help starting your life together, so allow me this honour," George argued.

The two men argued back and forth Mitchell wanting to pay for the usage of the field, and the brigadier adamant that it should be his gift to the happy couple.

Eventually their argument was interrupted by Lady Sarah and Miss Beaumont, who had finished two pots of tea whilst waiting on the gentlemen, and had grown concern that the two men were still cloistered in the study.

"Gentlemen, I am sure that this disagreement over whether the land should be a gift or some compensation should be offered is terribly important, but the shadows are lengthening," Lady Sarah said dryly to quiet the two men.

"We shall take this up another time then," Mitchell Claydon said as he rose from his chair.

"No, you shall not," Miss Beaumont said sternly. "Brigadier, we shall humbly accept your gift of the use of your land for our wedding feast."

Mr Claydon opened his mouth to argue with his intended, but she shot him a dark look that kept him silent.

"Wonderful. I will have Cooky set to work on your feast at once. She will have a great deal to plan. If you let her know how many people to expect, that will be perfect," the brigadier said.

"You are too generous, brigadier," Miss Beaumont began.

"And it is very much appreciated, I am sure," Lady Sarah said with an amused smile. Miss Beaumont nodded her head. She understood now why the two men had spent so long arguing, but she also knew that it would not be a fruitless endeavour to argue against the generosity of the brigadier with Lady Sarah there to support him.

"With that settled, please accept these invitations for our wedding," Miss Beaumont said as she reached into her bag and pulled out five envelopes addressed to different members of the household.

Chapter 4

Mrs Bosworth was relieved when the morning of departure finally arrived. Though it had only been a few days since the trip had been planned, the household had been in uproar packing for the trip and at the same time, preparing for the wedding of Mr Claydon and Miss Beaumont.

With Cooky and Bosworth out of the house, Mrs Bosworth could take control of the house once more and bring things back to the orderly normality that ruled the efficient running of the household.

Two carriages had been prepared for the journey as the dogs and Baker boys were now joining the expedition. Lee and Stanley had discovered the trip to Brighton and insisted that they be allowed to come along.

The puppies, Cooky, Bosworth and the Baker boys were to travel in one carriage, and Lady Sarah, Sylvia, the brigadier, Pattinson and Mr Hunter were to travel in the other carriage. The doctor and Richard Hales would travel down separately and meet their friends at the house that Mrs

Bosworth had rented for their holiday.

Harald and Black Guy, Mr Hunter and Lady Sarah's horses, were to be left behind at Grangeback to be cared for by the stable hands. The journey would not be a short one as Brighton was almost 270 miles away from Stickleback Hollow.

But they would change horses twice a day at different inns, and arrangements had been made for them to stay with different families along the route. It took them four hours to travel between the inns to change the horses, and they would change back at the same places on the return journey to return the horses to their rightful owners.

It took three days before the tired travellers arrived at the house Mrs Bosworth had arranged for them to rent for the holiday and the housekeeper for the property was most anxious when they did arrive.

"Oh we expected you hours ago, I thought something terrible had happened!" she said flustered and fussy as the drivers opened the doors to the carriages and the dogs all leapt out. "Oh my, so many animals."

"You must be Mrs Holbrook," the brigadier said as climbed out of he carriage and turned to help the ladies.

"Yes, sir, I am. Your housekeeper told me that you were bringing your own cook and your butler with you," Mrs Holbrook replied.

"We have indeed, my butler Bosworth is this rather distinguished looking gentleman, and the beautiful woman with him is Cooky," George said warmly. "I am Brigadier Webb-Kneelingroach, this is my son, Mr Hunter Webb-Kneelingroach, my ward, Lady Montgomery Baird Watson-Wentworth, her companion, Sylvia and finally her two apprentices, Lee and Stanley Baker," he announced as he introduced the whole party and the drivers began to unload the luggage.

"You are all most welcome, I shall show you each to your rooms, but the baggage is not something that falls within my duties," Mrs Holbrook said stiffly.

"Surely you do not expect your guests of such high rank to carry their own baggage?" Bosworth scoffed with disgust.

"I am only paid to look after the house and stock the pantry for guests when they are coming. Anything else is up to the guests," Mrs Holbrook replied with a surly edge to her voice.

"We'll carry the bags, Bosworth," Lee volunteered and he and Stanley rush to be the first to grab one of the many bags that had already been removed from the carriages.

"And where is the stabling for the horses and the carriages?" Bosworth asked with a sneer, having taken an instant dislike to Mrs Holbrook.

"Round the back of the house. I am sure that the drivers will find their way," Mrs Holbrook said with a wave of her hand.

"And you have retained grooms to care for the horses?" Bosworth said, not letting her dismiss him so easily.

"Of course not, the drivers take care of the horses," Mrs Holbrook spat in reply.

"Madam, drivers drive the carriages, grooms take care of the horses. The two are not the same thing, and just as you are not paid to carry baggage, the drivers are not paid to carry for the horses. Engage two grooms at once," Bosworth instructed firmly, and Mrs Holbrook rounded on him with a face of thunder.

"It is quite clear you are not well acquainted with the ways of the south. I don't know how things are done in the north, but down here we do things differently," Mrs

Holbrook said with narrowed eyes.

"Utter rubbish," Mr Hunter growled, and Mrs Holbrook turned to look at the tall man with the intimidating presence.

"Excuse me, sir?" Mrs Holbrook said, looking offended.

"Mrs Bosworth sent instructions when she rented this property. There was to be two footmen and two grooms engaged along with a scullery maid, and the sums to cover their wages were paid on top of the price for the house. Engage them at once or I shall set off for London to speak with our solicitor and Scotland Yard," Mr Hunter threatened.

Mrs Holbrook looked between Mr Hunter and Bosworth with a helpless expression on her face. It was unclear whether she was simply trying to cheat her paying guests, or it was the owner of the house, but either way, she had no choice but to do as Mr Hunter had ordered.

"In the meantime, as there are no footmen to carry the baggage, it is your responsibility," Bosworth said and both Lee and Stanley looked crestfallen. They put the bags they had seized down and looked over at Lady Sarah for some indication of what they should do.

"The rooms, Mrs Holbrook," Lady Sarah said lightly. The housekeeper nodded and took the party inside.

Pattinson padded at his mistress' side, and the puppies followed him in a line, their noses held high in the air and their tails pointed up.

Cooky had not need to be shown to her room, she would make sure the Baker boys knew where she would be sleeping. Instead, she made her way through the house, looking for the kitchen.

As there were no grooms to care for the horse that night, Mr Hunter took on the responsibility and found that they were lacking in some of the most basic supplies for the stables. There was no hay for the horses to eat during the day, the straw for the bedding was damp and had mould growing on it, and the oats had been left so long, they had begun to seed.

Inside the house, the story was no better. Sylvia was shocked at how poorly Mrs Holbrook kept the house. There was a layer of dust over every surface and the linens had not been changed on the beds in quite sometime.

In the kitchen, the pantry was almost completely devoid of any food and Cooky could not even find the words to describe how dirty the grate was.

Mr Hunter made his way back to the house, the horses left in their traces and the drivers awaiting instructions.

Sylvia had made her way to the kitchen to speak with Cooky and Bosworth and that is where Mr Hunter found them.

"Disgraceful," is all that Cooky could say about the state of the house.

"Agreed, but what can be done?" Sylvia asked.

"I will go to London directly," Mr Hunter said.

"Though a direct course of action, sir, a more prudent course might be to ask for the address of the owner of this property and pay them a visit," Bosworth suggested.

"Or perhaps we go stay at an inn for the night and pass the bill to the owner for payment as the house is uninhabitable," Sylvia suggested.

"The house must be made right before the morning though," Cooky sighed.

"It must indeed, but that would require a force of nature like Mrs Bosworth to accomplish such a feat," Mr Hunter replied.

"Bosworth, take Mr Hunter to find whatever help you

can in the local area. Perhaps one of the pubs will have people willing to work for a short time to clean up this mess," Cooky said thoughtfully.

"And what shall you and I do?" Sylvia asked.

"We shall set out in search of supplies. There must be a butcher and green grocer close by at the very least. Hopefully there will also be a dry good store too," Cooky said as she began to write out a list of everything they would need.

"What do we tell Lady Sarah, the brigadier, and the Baker boys?" Mr Hunter asked.

"That we will be back soon. They will need to be here for Doctor Hales and Richard arriving. We will take the coaches and pay an inn to stable the horses tonight. The drivers can lodge at the inn, and return here tomorrow when everything has been set to rights," Bosworth said firmly.

"Very well, I will go inform Lady Sarah of what is happening, perhaps the Baker boys can distract Mrs Holbrook for a time with the dogs," Sylvia said with a slight smile.

Lee and Stanley relished the opportunity to cause some chaos to cover the actions of their friends. The puppies were always willing accomplices in any hi-jinx due to their playful nature. Pattinson was good at keeping the puppies in line, and even better at sleeping whilst watching over Lady Sarah.

Lady Sarah elected to wait in the garden for Richard and Doctor Hales to arrive whilst the brigadier looked over the house to see if there was anything that the others had missed in their assessment of the property.

The doctor and Richard arrived an hour after the two groups had departed and Lady Sarah greeted them from the front garden where she had found a wrought iron table and chairs where she could sit and read whilst she waited for the others. Pattinson had curled up on the grass close by and gone to sleep.

It did not take long for her to inform the new arrivals of the situation at the house, and, as Richard had driven the coach himself, decided to stay at the inn that night with the horses and would come back the following day once things had been settled.

The doctor sat in the garden with Lady Sarah and they were joined by the brigadier, who reported that Mrs Holbrook was being kept amply occupied by the Baker boys and the puppies and would be unlikely to interfere in the efforts of Sylvia, Cooky, Bosworth and Mr Hunter to fix her many oversights.

Sylvia and Cooky returned to the house first with arms laden with food, soaps and a small amount of cooking equipment. Richard had ferried them back from the shops and then returned to fetch Bosworth and Mr Hunter from their errand finding staff and supplies for the stables.

Mrs Holbrook did not live at the house and left as the clock struck 6 o'clock, clearly frustrated and worn out by the work of the Baker boys and the puppies.

Cooky set to work preparing dinner with gusto whilst Sylvia and Bosworth cleaned the dining room and changed all the linens in the bedrooms.

Mr Hunter took the Baker boys out to the stables to help get rid of the rotting and putrid straw and oats, clean and prepare the stables for the horses arriving the next day.

After dinner, the brigadier looked over the list of people that would be arriving the following morning to take care of the house, and the doctor and Lady Sarah took charge of unpacking all the cases.

Sylvia drew hot baths for everyone and by the time the clock struck 10 o'clock in the evening, each of their party had done a hard days' work.

Cooky was the first to bed and the first awake the next morning. The rest of the food that they had ordered for their stay would be arriving early and there was the breakfast to prepare.

Bosworth rose not long after to greet the staff as they arrived and instruct them in their duties.

Richard and the drivers brought the horses and carriages back to the house and the horses were bedded down in the stables and the drivers went to inspect the paddock for any problem plants of dangers to the horses before they were let out to exercise later on.

By the time Mrs Holbrook arrived at the house, it was a hive of activity and being run efficiently by Bosworth. The housekeeper was astounded and found she could do nothing to establish herself as the authority in the house, nor was she needed. But rather than leave the house to Bosworth's expert care, she stayed and interfered in every thing that she could. Getting under Cooky's feet, ordering the grooms about when the drivers and Bosworth's backs were turned. She yelled at the scullery maid and made a nuisance of herself.

Mrs Bosworth was in the midst of organising a full spring clean of the manor. She had attempted to do so when the household had gone to Chillington Hall, but their time away was so short, they had not gotten far with it.

With the promise now of several weeks away in Brighton, Mrs Bosworth had the time and staff prepared to take on the task.

All the rugs were taken out of the house and hung on lines so the dust could be beaten out of them, the floors were scrubbed by maids on their knees, and all of the windows were flung open so that the dust being stirred up in the house could escape to the outdoors.

Mrs Bosworth was carrying out her third lot of laundry to hand on the line when a visitor called at the manor.

Mr Oliver Henry Brown was surprised to see the hive of activity around the manor and even more surprised to learn the household had left for Brighton for the foreseeable future.

"Do you know where they are staying?" Mr Brown asked innocently.

"At White House, in the centre of the town," Mrs Bosworth said.

"Thank you, I shall leave you to your cleaning," Mr Brown said and departed. That afternoon, he called upon his cousins at Tatton Park and the following morning, Mr Brown, Mr Thomas Egerton, Mr Edward Egerton, Mrs Charlotte Egerton and Mrs Mary Egerton were all piled into the two carriages, along with Thomas and Edward's twin younger siblings, Charlotte and Charles, all bound for White House, and Brighton.

Chapter 5

The atmosphere around White House was rather tense as Mrs Holbrook did her best to undermine Cooky and Bosworth at every turn. The brigadier had attempted to intervene and was told in no uncertain terms by Cooky, that it was not a battle for him to fight.

To avoid the growing tensions, and allow Bosworth and Cooky the privacy to deal with matters properly, the party decided to visit the beach front and to walk along by the sea.

Sea bathing was something that had been discussed, but as the beaches were segregated for men and women, Mr Hunter had not been keen on the idea. So for their first trip to the seaside from the house, the group decided to walk along the promenade and head to the pier.

It was not an impressive structure, but the chain pier was a popular landmark. Passenger ferries ran from the pier to Dieppe in France, and there were kiosks set up along it and confectionery stalls that made it quite the attraction.

Sylvia had also never been to Brighton and found, like Lady Sarah, the sea front to be a wonder to behold.

Lined up along the women's beach were bathing contraptions on wheels with horses and strong men waiting to tow them out into the waves.

In the surf there were bathing contraptions with canvas stretch over the water, some without, but each pulled to different locations for women to bathe at in privacy.

The men's beaches were filled with men in woollen bathing garments lining the sand and playing in the surf. There were even pontoons that had people serving cups of tea and small sandwiches from in the waves with swimmers gathered about them, enjoying the fine weather and cool sea waters.

The promenade was also crowded with people making their way between the shops selling bathing suits, towels, souvenirs, small buckets and gardening trowels that were being used by the men to create sand structures on the beach.

It was a hive of activity that one had to experience to believe. There was even an massage house that had once belonged to Doctor Brighton that offered champo head massages.

Richard and Sylvia walked side-by-side, Doctor Jack Hales and the brigadier walked not far behind them, the four of them separating from Lady Sarah, Pattinson, Mr Hunter, the Baker boys and the three puppies.

The puppies were all on very short leads, but Pattinson was so well trained he did not need a lead. He trotted at Lady Sarah's heel and showed no desire to be anywhere else.

Lee and Stanley held the leads for the puppies and were just as excitable and full of energy as the small dogs were.

At every new sight they were running over to take it in. By the time they reached the pier, they rushed off and were lost in the crowd. Mr Hunter made to call out after them, but Lady Sarah put her hand on his arm and said,

"Let them go explore, there are so few times when we get to experience this kind of place, and at their age, they should seize all the joy they can," she smiled.

Mr Hunter smiled back and nodded that she was right. The two walked down the pier together, with Pattinson between them.

Mr Hunter thought about offering his arm to the lady but there was something about the positioning of the dog that told him it was not the best to try and extend the intimacy of the moments they were sharing.

They walked slowly, stopping at the kiosks to see what was on offer, and finally reached out the end of the pier so that they could stare out at the sea.

It was far more peaceful at the end of the pier than it was where people were massing to visit the fortune tellers, the confectioners, and all the other attractions.

Lady Sarah took a deep breath and filled her lungs with the clean sea air. She knew the reason that the others had conspired to leave the pair alone but she had been hoping to avoid such a meeting for the first few days of the trip so that she could think on her answer a little more.

Mr Hunter cleared his throat, unsure of how to phrase all that he wanted to say. But before he could speak, Pattinson barked and moved away from Lady Sarah's side and rushed over to the side of the pier.

Sarah and Alex frowned at one another and followed after the dog. Others on the pier were staring at the trio, starting a commotion that drew the attention of Sylvia and

Richard.

"What is it?" Sylvia asked as the pair rushed over.

"There's bodies in the water," Lady Sarah said as she looked over the side of the pier and in the surf were floating the bodies of six women and four children, all women and all of oriental descent.

"What do we do?" Richard asked.

"Go find your father and fetch the police," Mr Hunter replied and under his breath cursed whoever was responsible for the bodies.

Chapter 6

Richard moved quickly and the police arrived just as people began to panic on the pier. Lee, Stanley and the three puppies were doing their best to keep the people back from where Lady Sarah, Mr Hunter and Sylvia were all stood, each looking down at the bodies with disgust.

Pattinson was sat at Lady Sarah's feet. He was not barking, nor making any fuss, but keeping a watchful eye for anyone who might get to close to his mistress.

Boats were soon found to fish the bodies out of the water and the doctor and brigadier were waiting on the beach to examine the bodies. The advantage of knowing Doctor Hales was that he knew people everywhere that they seemed to go. Whether it was Buckingham Palace or a small tow in Wales, there would be an old family friend, a fellow doctor that admired Jack's work, or a friend from his days at university.

When all of the bodies were removed from the surf and the doctor had been able to look at the bodies, he had confirmed that the women and children were of Chinese origin, and that from his examination, they were young enough and nourished enough to not be dead from immediately obvious natural causes.

"But where did they come from to end up here?" Sylvia asked no one in particular.

"That would be one of two questions I intend to find the answer to," Lady Sarah said firmly.

"What is the other question you wish to ave answered?" Mr Hunter asked.

"Why they are dead," Lady Sarah replied.

The bodies at the beach brought an end to their first day at the beach. Though it had barely been a handful of hours since they had left the house, they had no choice but to return to it. The beaches had been closed for the investigation to comb them for evidence.

As they returned to White House, there was a new set of carriages drawing up at the house. Out of the two coaches came the Egertons and Mr Oliver Henry Brown.

As Mr Hunter laid eyes on his rival, her felt the sting of anger and a sense of betrayal that someone had given him enough information in order to be able to follow the party so far south.

"Lady Sarah! Oh what fun this shall be!" Charlotte exclaimed as the party entered the house and found the Egertons and Mr Brown in the sitting room.

"I am afraid our holiday will be far from fun," the brigadier sighed.

"What happened?" Thomas Egerton asked with a frown as he looked from one face to another.

"We found ten bodies in the water, it looks like they were murdered," Mr Hunter replied gruffly as he did his best to not glower at Mr Brown.

"Then there is a mystery to solve?" Mary asked with a groan in her voice.

"There is, but that should not impede your sea bathing," Lady Sarah insisted.

"Mary and I will let the rest of you talk, we are able to entertain and amuse ourselves with the delights of Brighton," Charlotte sighed, knowing that both Edward and Thomas would be more interesting in helping to solve whatever it was that Lady Sarah had stumbled over this time than in enjoying the sea.

"If you are sure," Edward said looking nervously at the two women.

"We are," Mary said and the pair stood as one and left the sitting room.

"My colleague will send word when the bodies have been sent to him. He will allow me to examine the bodies and we shall make a study of what caused their deaths. I will report back when I know more," the doctor said.

"What can be done in the meantime?" Mr Brown asked.

"Nothing. Until we know more about the women and children, and what killed them, we have nothing to investigate," Lady Sarah shrugged.

"Then let us enjoy one meal together before we are consumed by this mystery, and perhaps save Thomas and I from a scolding from our wives," Edward said with a grin.

"I shall have Cooky prepare something at once," the brigadier said in agreement.

"You shall have much more time than one meal. I will know nothing until tomorrow at the earliest, even once I begin my examinations," the doctor said.

"Then we shall at least be able to take in an afternoon of entertainment," Thomas said with glee.

It was an hour before the bodies arrived at the morgue and it was another hour before Doctor Hales was summoned to examine them.

With ten bodies to examine there was much to prepare and it would take a great deal of time to complete the examinations of each body.

The brigadier had accompanied the doctor to the morgue, keen to be away from the afternoon of running about Brighton. He had enjoyed the walk on the pier, but he was in no mood to be entertained by the distractions that appealed to the younger members of their party.

"It would be helpful to be able to first know where they have come from, but I doubt we shall find any documentation," the doctor sighed.

"They are Chinese," the brigadier said as he looked closely at each face, trying not to allow the age of the children to upset him.

"How the devil do you know that?" the doctor frowned at his friend.

"There is much you do not know of my time with the army, or recent events," George sighed. "But I can say without any doubt, these women and children are all Chinese. Farm folk too."

"I can accept that you would know their country of origin, but how can you know what their profession is?" the doctor frowned.

"Their skin. Granted they have been in the water for sometime, but those who work in the fields have more pigment in their skin. The weather can be harsh and hot, and cold and unforgiving, it shows in their skin," the brigadier replied.

"Then that is of some help. I will begin with those observations in mind and see what else we can learn," the doctor sighed.

Chapter 7

The afternoon spent on the Brighton promenade was one that Lee and Stanley Baker would remember for years to come.

It was one filled with new experiences for them. The dogs remained with Sylvia, who had no intention of taking the waters, and Richard who did not wish to leave her on her own. The rest of the party went down to the beach. The men to their beach, and Lady Sarah, Charlotte and Mary to the ladies beach.

Charlotte and Mary went into their bathing contraptions first and were pulled out into the water, but Lady Sarah had no intention of swimming, instead she waited until Charlotte and Mary were both in the water before she left the beach and went in search of information.

There was a small Salvation Army chapel that she had spotted during their time walking the promenade, and it was there that she had decided to go.

It was not a fancy place, a simple hall that had chairs

laid out facing a lectern. There was a small kitchen that was used to prepare meals for the poor and homeless, and an office above the hall.

A woman dressed in the uniform that clearly identified all members of the Salvation Army, met Lady Sarah as she opened the door.

"Good morning," the woman said brightly. "How can I serve you?"

"Good morning, I have come to ask about the women and children found floating by the pier," Lady Sarah said.

"Oh not again," the woman said crossly. "That was weeks ago."

"Excuse me?" Lady Sarah said with a look of horror. "Weeks ago? How many times has this happened?"

"What do you mean?" the woman asked with confusion.

"I found six women and four children floating by the pier this morning. You say that bodies were found in the same place weeks ago. How many times have bodies been found?" Lady Sarah said with urgency.

"Three times now," the woman sighed heavily.

"Can you tell me about the other times?" Lady Sarah

asked.

"No, I only have hearsay to share, but I will ask the Commissioner if he is willing to speak with you about them," the woman said and disappeared up the staircase to the office above the hall.

She returned a few minutes later and indicated that Lady Sarah should go up.

The office was small, cramped and had very little in the way of furniture or light, but it was functional. Behind the cheap pine desk, a small man with round spectacles sat.

"Good morning, you wanted to ask about the bodies?" he said with a sigh and disapproving look on his face.

"I do, but not out of a sense of gossip or morbid curiosity you understand. I want to find out why these women and children are being killed and put a stop to it," Lady Sarah explained.

"Is that so," the commissioner said with interest and studied Lady Sarah intently for a few moments. "Very well, please sit down, Lady -" he said, leaving the inflection to allow Lady Sarah to introduce herself.

"Lady Montgomery Baird Watson-Wentworth," Lady Sarah said as she sat.

"Ah, now your questions make sense," the Commissioner said with a smile. "My name is Commissioner Jonnes Smith, I believe you know my brother."

"I do indeed, though I am surprised that my identity has brightened your mood. I was under the impression that the Chief Constable did not approve of my actions in his arena," Lady Sarah said with a wry grin.

"My brother has always wished to be glorified. It is one of his greater character flaws, and a smart woman, able to solve mysteries that others cannot is something that can be quite threatening to a man like that. I, on the other hand, would much rather have an end to death and crime, no matter who finds and stops the culprits," the commissioner explained.

"Then you would be willing to speak with me about these women and children that are washing up here?" Lady Sarah asked hopefully.

"Indeed, I am. The bodies first started appearing around six months ago. To begin with it was only one or two. We dismissed them as people falling off ships and drowning. The seas in the channel are often rough and it would not be beyond the realms of possibility for a careless passenger on a ship to fall overboard. But as more and more women and children began to be found, it became clear that there was a far more sinister pattern to the bodies appearing," the commissioner explained.

"Your colleague said that there had been only three instances of bodies washing up," Lady Sarah said with a frown.

"Three times when so many bodies have washed up, but there have been over twenty cases of dead bodies washing up on or near to the beach," the commissioner sighed and shook his head sadly.

"And you have a theory about where they have come from?" Lady Sarah asked.

"I have. I believe that they are women and children that have been sold into slavery and are being brought into this country to work in the brothels here," the commissioner said darkly.

"Children?" Lady Sarah asked with disgust.

"I am sad to say that powerful men and women both take pleasure in children. It is disgusting and depraved, but while we can protect the children of our own nation to an extent, and the work of dear Mrs Fry continues to help in that regard, children that are being brought from overseas, we are almost powerless to do anything for," Commissioner Jonnes Smith replied helplessly.

"It is bad enough that women should suffer such indignities, but children? We must act at once," Lady Sarah said forcefully, rather surprising the commissioner.

"I wish that we could, but we know almost nothing about where they are coming from, least of all why they are being thrown into the sea. Are they dead before they are thrown overboard, are they still alive when it happens, but they are not longer useful? There are many unanswered questions, and the police here are of little help. They do not see the pattern or the danger," Commissioner Jonnes Smith explained with a heavy heart.

"Then I shall do what must be done. I may not be able to remove despicable appetites from society, but I will remove this menace," Lady Sarah said firmly as she rose to her feet.

"My lady, you are far more astounding than you realise. Do not lose this fire or spark that you have brought with you from the Indian shores. Society here will try to smother it, try to force you to be seen and not heard. Be like

Mrs Fry and make a difference," the commissioner urged her as he stood to escort her to the door.

"You paint a very bleak picture of society," Lady Sarah said looking at the commissioner with concern.

"We are a fallen world and a fallen people, my lady. There is only one redemption, one hope, one light. He can be seen in the every day kindnesses that bring a bright spot to the days of the downtrodden, and He works through the hands of people like you. Society is a bleak place, but when hearts like yours do what is right, the days become a little brighter," Commissioner Jonnes Smith said, and Lady Sarah could see the passion in his eyes. He was a man of God, he was a spiritual leader before anything else, and she couldn't help but admire his faith.

"I shall do what I can to make this right. The rest, I leave up to you," Lady Sarah smiled in return.

"And I shall not rest until this plague of immorality is stopped!" the commissioner declared. "It has been a pleasure talking with you, my lady. You have renewed my fire and hope. I wish you luck in your endeavours."

"Commissioner, luck is a pagan belief," Lady Sarah said with mock-shock. "Besides, I do not believe in luck."

Chapter 8

The doctor was left alone with the bodies at the morgue. His connections were something he had made over the course of his career, and though he had not intentionally created a useful network that would help in the caring of injured friends, or allow him access to dead bodies, and medical facilities that could help with the solving of murders, it was certainly helpful now.

Jack Hales preferred to work alone. His son's decision to take a sabbatical from his studies and work with him in Stickleback Hollow was something that the doctor was looking forward to. For autopsies, though, it was best that his son be elsewhere and not under his feet.

There was a time for teaching and a time for focus, and this was a time for focus. There were details to look for that would tell the doctor a great deal, and trying to explain the process whilst observing those details would invariable lead to something being overlooked, or a key detail being missed.

As the bodies were all of drowning victims, the good doctor decided to begin his examination with the lungs of the victims. If they had truly drowned, there would be water in the throat and lungs that had caused the women and children to asphyxiate.

He cracked over the chest of the first body and carefully removed the heart and placed it to one side to examine later. Next he removed the lungs and placed them on the workbench to cut open. He sliced into the tissue and cut until he could open the lungs to look inside.

As he cut the lungs open he saw at once two things. One, there was no water in the lungs, meaning that the woman he was examining had died before she had been put into the sea; and two, the woman had been sick with tuberculosis. The paler sections of inflammation on the lungs coupled with the extensive caseous necrosis of the tissue were clear signs the woman had been suffering with the disease for quite some time before she died.

He continued his examination and found that she had a cracked skull and a large haematoma, suggesting to the doctor that she had been killed by a hefty blow to the head.

Once he had finished examining the first woman, he

moved on to the second woman, and the third, he examined every body he could that had been fished out of the sea in recent times and found that all of them had tuberculosis and all had been killed by similar blows to the head.

"To be brought so far from home only to be murdered and thrown into the sea," the doctor sighed to himself and shook his head. "At least you were not drowned." he comforted himself with the thought but still felt uneasy at what forces could possibly be at work that would have snatched young women and children from their homeland only to see them murdered on the voyage.

He tidied up after himself, cleaning the tools and making sure that the organs were returned to the bodies and he had thoroughly washed too. Not all doctors washed their hands or cleaned their implements, but it was a matter of pride with Jack Hales, and a mark that he had finished for the day.

He made sure that he had made extensive medical notes to pass on to his colleagues, and then he penned a note to one of his contacts in the Foreign Office, describing what he had found and requesting assistance at their earliest convenience.

He would send the runner that the coroner paid to deliver messages to deliver the note to the Foreign Office building next to Horse Guards. But that was the least of his concerns. He sat and brooded for a moment before deciding that his work was not done for the day, and set off to the Royal College of Physicians.

Chapter 9

The brigadier was not surprised when he say Lady Sarah stood on the promenade above the men's beach. Her hair was perfectly dry and it was clear even from a distance that she had not taken to sea bathing.

"Where have you been?" he asked after he had changed and walked to meet with his ward.

"To speak to the Salvation Army. Did you know that Captain Jonnes Smith's brother is the Commissioner of the chapter here?" Lady Sarah said innocently.

"No, what an interesting discovery. What else, pray tell, did you learn?" the brigadier asked, his tone slightly weary.

"That this is the third instance of bodies washing up in the last few weeks," Lady Sarah said solemnly.

"Only you, my dear ward, could go to the seaside and find a mystery to solve," the brigadier sighed and knew that the sea-bathing would have to wait.

Lee and Stanley Baker had seen Lady Sarah talking to

the brigadier and had rushed to change and join them, Pattinson hot on their heels.

"There are women and children washing up dead on our shores, and no one is doing a thing about it," Lady Sarah said with a shake of her head. "I cannot ignore that."

"You are right, of course, I shall take action at once and go directly to Scotland Yard," the brigadier replied.

"But that will take you the better part of the day," Lady Sarah frowned.

"And it shall be a day well spent if I can elicit even the smallest amount of help from the peelers, it shall be a day well spent," the brigadier replied. "I shall meet you tonight at the house. Until then, please try to be safe." he said with a wry smile.

"What can we do to help?" Lee Baker asked with excitement as the brigadier made his way down the promenade.

"You can accompany me. We are going in search of a ship, or at least we are going in search of where a ship carrying Chinese women and children might be," Lady Sarah said to the two boys, and Pattinson barked his approval.

"Does that mean we can go back to the pier?" Stanley

asked with excitement.

"Perhaps we should. I believe that we may need to visit the Fishing Quarter though. The fishermen would know where ships make port and the tides that would help us narrow down which port," Lady Sarah mused.

"Where is the Fishing Quarter?" Lee asked as he scratched his head.

"I believe it is in front of the Old Ship Hotel," Lady Sarah said and set off in the direction of the pier.

The Old Ship Hotel was a short walk from where they were and the break in the bathing beaches to the fishing waters was quite stark in contrast. The beaches were gravel and shell with stairs and slips and a high wall separating the fishing quarter from the bathing beaches.

There were a handful of boats on the slips, though most were clearly out at sea plying their trade. There was a group of weather beaten men talking as they smoked at the top of one of the staircases down to the slips below.

"Excuse me, sirs, might I ask you a question?" Lady Sarah asked as she, Pattinson and the Baker boys approached the four men.

The men looked up with a look of annoyance, but

seeing the young and beautiful lady approaching with two boys and a dog in tow, they held any rude comments they might have made.

"Yes, my lady?" the oldest looking of the four men said.

"No doubt you have heard about the bodies that have been washing up on the beaches," Lady Sarah said and received nods from the four men. "We are trying to find out what has been happening to the poor women and children."

"About time someone did. Poor blighters," a man with no teeth said.

"What is your question? We don't know much about it," the youngest looking man said with a shrug.

"Where would ships that might be carrying them dock?" Lady Sarah asked and the four men looked thoughtful for a time.

"From the look of their clothing, they were not passengers of the ships that dock at the pier," the fourth man said.

"No, looked like poor workers, like those in Limehouse in London," the man with no teeth spoke again.

"Limehouse?" Lady Sarah frowned.

"It's the Chinese district where the Chinese sailors all live. Poor men but hard workers," the oldest man explained.

"But it is not somewhere that ships would dock?"

"No, it is not my lady, but Shoreham would be," the fourth man said.

"Shoreham?" Lady Sarah asked.

"Shoreham-by-Sea, it's a town to the west of here. Been around since the Romans, but it's got a lot of shipbuilding yards and shipping. Not too many passenger ships though. But if the women and children are poor, they might be cargo on ships coming from China," the youngest man explained.

"That is extremely helpful, thank you gentlemen," Lady Sarah said, and she reached into her purse to pull out a guinea for each of the men.

"No, my lady, we cannot accept that," the oldest man tried to refuse her generosity.

"You work hard to earn a living and have helped me with your hard earned knowledge. It is only right that the value of such knowledge should be recognised," Lady Sarah smiled. The four men were at a loss of how to respond. Lee and Stanley smiled at the four men as Lady Sarah bid them goodbye.

"Don't worry, she does that," Lee grinned and the four men were left blessing the mysterious lady that had paid a guinea for the answer to a single question.

"Is there something that has upset you, your ladyship?" Stanley asked as he hurried to keep pace with his mentor.

"There is a community of Chinese sailors in London, but the bodies washing up on the beaches are women and children. Why are there no men?" Lady Sarah asked more of herself than of the two boys.

"Maybe the men are all working on the ships?" Lee offered.

"Then why are there women and children on the ships at all?"Lady Sarah wondered aloud.

Stanley looked at Lee who simply shrugged. They were used to listening to the grown ups talk, having ideas and then going off on their own to discover something interesting, but now they were apprenticed to Lady Sarah, their role would be quite different to what it was before. They were boys that were becoming men, and the idea was more than a little terrifying to the pair.

"Are the children all girls?" Stanley asked, causing Lady Sarah to stop mid-stride.

"We must go to the Salvation Army at once," Lady Sarah announced and hurried off, her stride twice as quick as before, Pattinson having to trot briskly to keep up with her.

Commissioner Jonnes Smith was happy to see Lady Sarah again so soon, but there was little cordiality in how quickly she jumped to her question.

"Have all the children been girls?" Lady Sarah asked.

The commissioner frowned and thought for a moment.

"Yes, they were all girls," he replied slowly.

"Then why is it only women and girls, and no men and boys?" Lady Sarah asked and the room was held in a stunned silence, as no-one assembled could answer.

Chapter 10

The absence of the brigadier, Pattinson and the Baker boys was soon noticed by the men on the beach, and the remaining men all quickly dressed and made their way down the promenade to await the women.

Sylvia was the first to emerge, followed by Charlotte, and Mary last. The group was beginning to worry about where Lady Sarah was when Pattinson's bark alerted them to Lady Sarah and the Baker boys returning.

"Where have you been?" Mr Hunter asked with a frown.

"Learning about the sea ports close by and as much as I can about the victims," Lady Sarah replied simply. Sylvia let out a short laugh, which earned dark looks from Mr Hunter.

"This is supposed to be a holiday. A time to relax, not investigate mysteries," Mr Hunter sighed as the plans he had in head for this holiday were fast turning to dust before his eyes.

"You sound just like your father," Lady Sarah replied

dryly.

"What did you discover?" Sylvia asked, causing Mr Hunter to glower more.

"That all the bodies are women and girls, there is not a man or boy among them. That this has happened multiple times. There is a Chinese community in Limehouse in London. and that there is a bustling shipping port and shipyard at Shoreham-By-Sea that could be where the ships that lost these souls were sailing to," Lady Sarah listed off the major points of what she had learned.

"And all of that whilst we played in the sea," Charlotte said with an impressed smile.

"Which is why we came," Mr Hunter said pointedly.

"You cannot expect her to turn her back on those in need," Mr Brown argued, sensing a chance to prove himself the more supportive of the two men and the more suitable man for marriage.

"They are not in need, they are dead. We cannot help the dead, save to bury them," Mr Hunter retorted.

"But what about those who are not yet dead?" Mr Brown replied, only half-thinking through the statement before he made it

"All of the other people on the planet? Lady Sarah has a brilliant mind, but she is not the saviour of the world," Mr Hunter scoffed.

"What if there are other women and children that need help that are not yet dead?" Mr Brown rephrased his statement.

"And what of the danger? What of risking her life yet again for the sake of a mystery? You have not been here long enough to know how many times she has nearly died, been kidnapped, locked away in an asylum, been wrongly imprisoned, and a whole other manner of terrible things that she should never have to endure," Mr Hunter raged and was beginning to garner strange looks from passers by.

"Enough, both of you. This fighting is not helping. If you cannot help, and wish to bicker like spoilt children, go back to Stickleback Hollow, and we shall solve this mystery without you," Lady Sarah snapped.

"Very well, I shall stop," Mr Hunter sighed.

"As will I," Mr Brown agreed.

"Very well, then the pair of you and Richard, Thomas and Edward should all go to Shoreham and search the port for any ships that might have carried the women. Men will go unnoticed there, women and children would only draw attention to themselves, which will hopefully work in our favour and someone would have noticed any Chinese women or children," Lady Sarah explained and the five men all nodded in agreement.

"Where has my father gone?" Mr Hunter asked.

"To Scotland Yard to fetch help," Lady Sarah replied.

"Very well, then to the port we will go," Mr Hunter agreed.

"And where shall we go?" Mary asked.

"We are bound for Scotland Yard to collect the brigadier and then to Limehouse, though it might be best if you and Charlotte were to wait at the house for Doctor Hales. He will not know where any of us have gone," Lady Sarah said.

"Very well, we shall await you all at the house," Charlotte said with pleasure. The idea of investigating did not appeal to her, but sitting in a warm house, reading a book, seemed like an excellent way to help the investigation.

Chapter 11

ary and Charlotte returned to the house that had been rented for their holiday, in order to await the doctor's return.

Lady Sarah, Sylvia, the Baker boys, and Pattinson rode in their carriage to London, stopping at Scotland Yard to collect the brigadier.

He had been frustrated for much of the day, but was glad that Lady Sarah had been able to uncover so much for them to investigate whilst Scotland Yard mobilised. He wished, in part, that Constable Evans had come with them now, but that could not be helped.

Limehouse was a run down area of the city that had become the centre of the Chinese sailor community. There were tea shops that Lady Sarah had to force herself to walk past rather than calling in, silk shops that had beautiful displays in the windows, and opium dens in a number that seemed excessive to Sylvia.

It lay on the Limehouse Causeway and had existed for

quite sometime. The majority of the people living in the community were men. There were a handful of women that worked in the teashops, but for the most part they were older women, some of them the mothers of the sailors. Others were related to the owners of the opium dens, tea shops, and silk shops.

But the lack of young women and children in the area was immediately noticeable.

"Do you suspect that the women and children are being carried as passengers or as cargo?" the brigadier asked as the group explored the Limehouse community.

"I don't know," said Lady Sarah. "It is possible that they've been treated as cargo. They were certainly cast aside easily enough."

"But what kind of human being would do such a thing?" asked the brigadier. "Women and children are being treated as cargo for what reason? And to be cast aside so cruelly. Seems monstrous."

"We will have to wait to see what Dr Hales finds," Lady Sarah replied.

"Yes, hopefully he will have some answers to shed some light on some of these mysteries," the brigadier agreed.

Lee and Stanley Baker had been very quiet during all of this. Both of them knew that children were far more disposable in the wider world than the brigadier and Lady Sarah seemed to be aware of.

Noticing that the pair have not said anything. Lady Sarah turned her attention towards them.

"The two of you should know more about this than anyone else," she said.

"Your ladyship thinks too much of people. That they would have the same moral code that you do," Stanley Baker said. Lady Sarah frowned and felt she'd been insulted somehow. "It is not that you have unrealistic expectations of people." Stanley said but Lee interrupted him and said,

"Actually, it is that you have unrealistic expectations of people," Lee said under his breath, but then blushed as Lady Sarah had heard him.

"What does that mean?" Lady Sarah asked in a gentle voice, though she felt more than a little hurt.

"Have you ever visited a workhouse or poor house? Have you seen the conditions that children are expected to work and live in?"Lee asked.

"I will admit I have not," Lady Sarah answered

slowly.

"When we were quite young, and we discovered that our mother was not really our mother. We were quite upset and decided we might want to run away. Try and find our real mother," Stanley explained.

"We didn't get very far before mother found us, and by mother I mean, Angela Baker," Lee qualified.

"But after our attempt to run away, she decided to take us to show us what the poor houses looked like. The orphanages, the places where we could have ended up if we hadn't been taken in by her," Stanley explained.

"And what are these places like?" Lady Sarah asked slowly.

"The worst possible places for children to end up," Stanley shrugged. "Children are not loved there, they are a commodity. Something that can be bought and sold to the highest bidder, then worked to the bone. They are not allowed to make decisions about their own lives. People come to the workhouse looking for a child to send up a chimney to clean until they are too old or too big and get stuck in the brickwork. Looking for a new scullery maid to beat or worse. Some children run away, and just end up on the streets as pickpockets and thieves, and eventually end up hanging from a rope."

"Not all children are not valued in the way that you value them. People do not think of children the way that you do. I would say the same is true of most women as well, who are not born to your station, my lady," Lee said.

"Then you think that these women have been treated as nothing more than commodities, just like the children?" Lady Sarah asked the two boys. It took a moment before the two boys answered, but after they shared a hard look, they replied,

"Yes, that is exactly what we think," Stanley said.

"I see. I am sorry that the world is such a dark place. That you've seen so much of the darkness from such a young age," Lady Sarah said slowly.

"Do not feel sorry for us. We have a mother that loves us very dearly, who treats us as though we are her own flesh and blood. She took his in when she did not have to. We have wanted for nothing in our lives. She has given us more opportunities than we could ever have imagined before," Stanley smiled.

"When we told her we wanted to come and work for

you. She was clearly reticent to allow us to but she knew that it was something that we wanted and knowing it was something we wanted. She did not refuse it to us. She let us make our own decision and our own mistakes. She is the best mother that either of us could ever have asked for." Stanley said firmly.

"You do not regret your own mother giving you up?" Lady Sarah asked, feeling the moment that the words left her mouth that she had gone too far. The Baker boys looked at each other and considered their reply.

"No. Our lives could have been far worse with our a real mother. I think she knew that, which is why she gave us up, and with Miss Baker we've been happy. We now work for you. We have great adventures. I'm not sure we could ever have asked for anything more with our lives," Lee replied.

"Well, in that case, then I'm happy for you. I am glad that you feel so loved and so valued, and my heart breaks for the poor children that we have found in this harbour," Lady Sarah said sadly

"We should set about trying to find some people to talk to you will not get anywhere if we stand here all day," the Brigadier said trying to lighten the mood. His voice was gentle and the others nodded in agreement with the brigadier, and set off at quite a pace with Lee and Stanley forged ahead with the brigadier following close behind.

Lady Sarah paused for a moment and took a deep breath. Patterson licked her hand. She and instinctively reached out to rest her head on top of his head.

"Thank you boy," she said sadly, and wished that the world was a better place and swore that she would do all she could to protect the Baker Boys in the same way that Angela Baker had.

Chapter
12

The five men had a rather uneventful trip to Shoreham-by-the-Sea. Mr. Hunter and Mr. Brown had taken to ignoring each other. They had sat there, obstinately staring out of the opposite carriage window to where the other sat, something that the Egertons and Richard both found quite amusing. None had commented on it, though they had all shared looks and smiles behind hands at the way that their friends were behaving.

When they arrived at Shoreham-by-the-Sea it was not hard to find the bustling port that Lady Sarah had told them about.

There was a great deal of life there, more so than they had expected to find. Wandering down to the shipyard, they could see what great ships were being built. Huge vessels to carry cargo across the seas, to the far corners of the growing empire.

"It is a testament to the things that humans could accomplish when they put their minds to it. Now then,"

Thomas said, clapping his hands together. "We should split up into two groups. Edwin and I, we shall go and explore the shipbuilding yard. Try and find anyone who might know something about ships bound from China. I want to see if there are any boats being built indeed for Chinese merchants," he announced.

"Why only for Chinese merchants?" Richard asked,

"Do you think that someone other than the Chinese merchants might be responsible? A British merchant perhaps?" Edward asked with surprise.

"Do not think that the evils of men are restricted to any particular nation," Richard said carefully. "I have met enough men in our time to know that there are evil men. British Chinese, French, Russian, German, Indian, it does not seem to matter," Richard said sensibly. Mr. Hunter nodded his head in agreement.

"I do not think you should limit yourself to only Chinese merchants. The East India Company is dealing a lot in China. I would also investigate any ships that have been commissioned for them recently too," Mr Hunter suggested.

"Very well. We do not wish to shut down any avenue of investigation, for fear that Lady Sarah may scold us,"

Edward said jibbing at both Mr Hunter and Mr Brown.

"Then we merry three," Richard said. "We'll go to the shipping lanes. Well, not quite the shipping lanes, but the slips at least," he smiled.

"We will see if we can find any ships that have been bound from China to here that have come in with less cargo than they should have," Mr Hunter said.

"That is an excellent idea," Thomas agreed.

"Then it is settled. There will be off at once. We shall all return and meet here within two hours," Edward suggested opening his pocket in order to check the time.

"Two hours it is, if we have not find anything then we can search for a little longer. We do not wish to stay too late. If we missed dinner, Cooky would have something of a fit," Mr Hunter warned.

"Dear Cooky," Edwards said with a grin. "The Brigadier is a smart man to have brought her along, he couldn't live without her cooking."

"I dare say it is less that he could not live without her cooking," Mr Hunter said "and more that he could not guarantee what kind of cooking we would get here. In the state that the house was in when we first arrived, he showed immense forethought in bringing both Cooky and Bosworth with us."

Mr Brown had stayed oddly silent and seem not to wish to engage in the conversation. This suited Mr Hunter fine. Though the American seemed to be more annoyed with the Egerton's for leaving him with his rival than he was at actually having to do anything with Mr Hunter.

Edward and Thomas parted from the group with merely a backward glance and wide grins.

"How long have you known your cousins?" Richard asked.

"What do you mean 'known my cousins'?" Oliver asked with a frown.

"I do not mean as a known your cousins," Richard said. "They've been your cousin's for all your life. I imagine."

"They have," Mr Brown agreed.

"I mean, when you grow up overseas, you do not have the same relationship you might with cousins that live close at hand. It has been some time that you have met with them spoken with them written letters to them to the best," Richard explained.

"Sometime? Not very long," Mr. Brown said in reply.

"I see," replied Richard.

"What is it?" Mr Brown asked

"That you were unaware of their particular brand of humour I take it?" Richard smiled.

"Particular brand of humour?" Oliver asked.

"They have been like this since the school days they're quite mischievous, and sometimes do not understand that their humour is not necessarily anything other than being slightly cruel to another," Richard explained. "They will not understand that they have offended you unless you tell them in some instances."

"I see," Mr Brown replied. "I appreciate the explanation," he said somewhat sourly.

"Now come, we will make the best of today," Richard said clapping his hands. "And the two of you will learn to be fine friends before the end of it."

Mr Hunter at least nodded to acknowledge what Richard had said. Neither he nor Mr. Brown looked as though would ever be nothing other than rivals.

"Come now, gentleman. We have a mystery to solve," Richard said, and the three men set off towards the slips.

The docks where the slips were found were full of

activity. Ships were coming into the harbour, and steered over to the slips so that they could be unloaded and loaded. There were sailors all over the dockside working hard, not a single one looking up from their work as the three men passed.

The sounds of the shipyard at work were not all that dissimilar from the sounds of a busy city. The bustle seemed the same too, though there was a greater number of prostitutes lining the docks than even Mr Hunter had ever seen in one place.

All three men we're glad that Lady Sarah had suggested that they and not she visited the shipyard. The language that they had heard was offensive to all of their ears, and they could not imagine what effect it would have had on Lady Sarah. Though she also had seen prostitutes and the female form, Mr Hunter was especially glad that Lady Sarah did not have to witness the lewd displays that the female and male prostitutes were putting on to attract customers from the incoming ships.

With so many of them in one place, competition was fierce and whatever they had to do to gain the coin they needed to eat was what they would do, and it was not something that those from the more sheltered areas of life should have to witness.

After walking for a few minutes, and doing their best to avoid being accosted by the workers on the docks, they found a man who looked like he was in charge of a section of the shipping lanes, and asked him where the chips bound to and from China could be found.

The man was directing a particularly ignorant captain to the far end of the slips, and did not appear to take too kindly to interruption.

"Head to the east, far end of that row of slips, ask for a man called Mayfair," he said he turned his attention away from them and back to the ship that was on course to crash with a small sloop that was anchored in the middle of the path the captain was attempting to take.

The three men moved on through the dockyards and found the man called Mayfair. It took them quite a while as there were lots of men milling about and very few of them cared to stay to stop and speak with them.

When they found Mayfair he professed to be rather busy when presented with what looked like three gentleman making inquiries. The men who worked on the dockyards were not all reputable men, and when those that appeared to be from any form of official government department, force or men that had a journalistic air, there was an understanding that they were men to be ignored and avoided.

But the moment that coins were produced from pockets, Mayfair made the time as making a little extra money on the side for providing information was the only acceptable reason to speak with well-dressed outsiders.

"So what is it I can do for you gentleman?" Mayfair asked with a grin that revealed many missing teeth and a wretched smell from the ones that remained.

"Well we are interested in some ships from China," Richard explained.

"Interested how?" Mayfair asked with suspicion.

"Our fathers have all made investments with certain shipping companies," Richard lied.

"Is that so?" Mayfair said, not sounding convinced byt the story.

" Yes, they're concerned about their investments though. Certain ships have reported cargo losses," Alex replied, joining Richard in his lie.

"I see, and you're here to investigate those losses?"

Mayfair enquired, sounding more convinced.

"You can understand, sir, that we have a vested interest in such things," Mr. Brown said his American accent coming across very clearly, which seemed to clinch things with Mayfair.

"Indeed I can," said Mayfair "But this information does not come cheap."

Richard sighed he had expected as much, but had hoped that they would find someone willing to help them for nothing.

"Very well. For any information that you give us that allows us to help stem the losses our fathers are making, we shall each pay you one shilling. Agreed?" Richard asked with clear reticence.

"Oh, well then gentleman! Tell me what information I can provide to you!" Mayfair said with a greedy smile upon his. Three shillings for a short conversation and no heavy lifting was far more generous than he had expected the three men to be.

"We need the names of ships that are arriving from China that have less cargo on them than they should in the logs," Richard explained.

"I see," Mayfair said. "Oh they'll be fewer and far between gentleman." he seemed almost sarcastic when he spoke.

"Then most ships come in light on their cargo?" Richard asked.

"Seems to be the way of shipping, sir. Especially food items. What is it that's been brought in from China?" Mayfair asked with suspicion.

"Tea mostly, and some silks," Mr Hunter was quick to say.

"Then reputable merchants your fathers are," Mr Mayfair smiled. It seemed that there was a great deal of illegal activity that went on in the shipping industry that none of the men wanted to know more about.

"Oh, I'll see what my record show," Mayfair said and led the three men to a shall hut to look at the logs. "Oh now, that is interesting." he said after a short time pouring over some ledgers.

"What is it?" Mr. Brown asked.

"Well, there's two ships in particular that always seem to come in with light on their loads. And by light, I mean, very light on their loads. We always ask for a reason, just in case investors such as yourself, show up wanting to know what's happened. Generally there'll be a good reason for cargoes to be so short, but this spillage, storms, incorrect storage, none of that would cause such losses. As far as I can see," Mr. Mayfair said with a frown.

"That's very interesting indeed," Richard said thoughtfully.

"What are the names of these two ships?" Mr Hunter asked.

"Well, let me have a look. That information will cost you more than a shilling, though, gentleman," Mayfair said seriously. He knew full well that men willing to pay a shilling for a little information that might be useful would be willing to pay a lot for information that was very useful.

"How much?" Mr Brown sighed. He did not like or approve of paying good money to men like Mayfair for information.

"Gentlemen, let us not talk of money in such a sordid way," Mr Mayfair said in an insincere manner. "Let us just say that if this information is valuable to you, you will reward me with what you think your value should be," he held out his hand expectantly as he finished speaking.

Mr. Brown scoffed and turned up his nose intent to refuse such a thing, but both Richard and Mr Hunter put their hands into their pockets and pulled out three guineas each.

"What are you doing?" Mr Brown asked with incredulity.

"We need this information. Mr. Mayfair has it for two ships to be so light on their loads," Mr Hunter said. "It seems very worth paying such paying well for such information."

Richard nodded his agreement. Mayfair's eyes rounded wide with amazement at the amount of money sitting in his hand. He'd never held so much money so much money in his life, let alone had that much of his own money at anyone time.

"You gentleman are most generous," he said, doing his best to hide his surprise, but a greedy smile spread across his lips. "Well then, this clearly shows me you are serious in your intent to discover what has happened to your family investments. The ships in question the Jang Ji trawler and the Shang Shu. They both are in port at the moment in fact, over at the far end of the slips to the west. There's nothing more I can tell you about either ship, though. You might have better luck talking with the ship's captain. Or the crew. But I will warn you, with ships like that they're rarely British sailors. So you may not have all that much luck in communicating. You might get lucky as a few on the ships can speak English, but they might not be so ready to help. Good luck to you gentleman. And if I can be of any further assistance, please don't hesitate to ask," Mayfair said.

"We shall bear that in mind," Richard said and the three men nodded their good days to Mayfair. They began to make their way back to head to the west of the ships.

"We should not be dealing with swindlers like that," Mr Brown said as the three walked away, and he was certainly we're out of earshot.

"That is just not how the world works, sadly," Richard replied.

"The three of us are very blessed to be in the positions we are in. And men like Mayfair, maybe rather sordid in their greed, but it's only because they have nothing to begin with. Men who are lucky like us, and still hold even more wealth for the detriment of others, they are men that we should not be dealing with," Mr Hunter replied.

Mr. Brown shook his head. But the point was well made and clearly something he'd not considered before. He fell silent as he began to reflect on some of the people that he knew, not only in England, but in the United States as well and their approach to money. There were those who were selfish and greedy, and those who were generous and kind.

He thought about the men that his father did business with and how those that had plenty of money but were greedy with it made for poor business partners, whereas those who were generous and kind may make some poor business decisions, but on the whole were much better long term partners.

He did not like admitting that Mr Hunter was right, but he could not escape the fact that, though his rival for the affections of Lady Sarah, Mr Hunter was an excellent judge of human character and his insights into the minds of men would be invaluable when questioning the ships crew.

Chapter
13

The day exploring the Limehouse community had proven many things. But more than anything else, the community proved to be a rather intimidating place for both Lady Sarah and Sylvia.

As they walked past men in the street, they openly gawked and stared, causing the two women to feel most self-conscious, and even caused Lady Sarah to begin to wish she was invisible. Some of the men shouted things in Chinese that caused the Brigadier to turn angrily and shout in reply. His Cantonese was not as good as his Mandarin, but given the time he had spent in the Canton region, it enabled him to communicate with people most effectively.

The sight of a man such as the brigadier returning insults in their native tongue was enough to send most of the men scurrying away without a moment's pause, but those that did not seem to be scared by the brigadier, soon were by the growling Japanese hunting dog.

Pattinson could not understand language, but he

understood tone and body language and the dog did not approve of the way that the men were acting towards his mistress.

Lee and Stanley stayed close to Sylvia and Lady Sarah, neither boy wishing to see the ladies hurt by being in such a place.

The amount of opium dens was something that both surprised and upset Lady Sarah, more so than any of the catcalls and behaviour of the men of the area.

She had seen the effects of such things living in India. Men who became involved with the drug were often changed beyond belief.

Silvia understood the desire for escapism that such a caused men and women to take opium, but the toll it took on the lives and that it merely masked the pain people suffered, pain that festered and was never dealt with, was something she found distasteful.

People became stuck in their pain, in an inescapable loop of needing to escape with the drug that became less effective every time they took it, so more was needed until finally they took so much that their bodies could no longer cope with the abuse.

Sylvia was even more glad than ever that Lady Sarah had found her before she had sunk to the level of opium addiction when she had been cast out onto the streets.

The brigadier, upon seeing the women's reaction to the lighthouse community explained,

"The reason that it is so rampant in China it's not because they grow it. It's because we import it to them. And when I say we, I mean the East India Company. When we first began trading with China there was an awful lot that we found that we needed from them including silks, teas, things like that. But the Chinese were not interested in buying anything from us. They were only interested in taking our silver. After a time we found that our wealth was slowly being bled away to the Chinese Empire. The Emperor didn't seem to care. We were infidels. We are all lower forms of life to those of the chosen Chinese. And so we needed to find other ways to recoup our losses. Opium proved to be the most successful at stemming the tide. If the Chinese had been more willing to act as trading partners for mutual benefit, then perhaps this evil would not have been released in such a fashion. But it is now too late to put the genie back in it's bottle," he shrugged.

"If it does not grow in China, where does it come from?" Sylvia asked.

"It is grown in India, and we then package it and ship it over to the Canton region. It is illegal in China now, but it doesn't stop the Chinese people from engaging in it," the brigadier continued.

"Why is that?" Lady Sarah asked.

"They make a lot of money out of it. They get an escape from the rigidity of their lives there. It's a highly addictive drug. Once someone starts taking it, they are an addict for life," the brigadier sighed.

"Is that why you were called away so suddenly?" Lady Sarah asked.

"Yes, there was a situation in Canton, and it was done for the good of the Empire," Brigadier George Webb-Kneelingroach for a moment looked more serious than Lady Sarah had ever seen him.

"But not for the good of the people," Lady Sarah replied.

"Sometimes you have to weigh the good of harming a few for the benefits of many," the Brigadier said flatly in reply. Silvia nodded in agreement, but said nothing.

Lady Sarah did not approve of such actions, but she began to understand a little more the difference between those that had to make choices for others. There were hard choices that meant others would be harmed, but the majority would not. She could not imagine being in such a position and knew that Lady de Mandeville often had to make such decisions.

She was almost certain that her parents were casualties of such actions, and though she had loved her mother and father dearly, the longer she had spent in England and coming to understand the world, the more certain she was they had been ill used by Fitzwilliam and ultimately, their deaths could have been avoided if not for the games of power that were played out of the view of most of society.

But now was not a time to dwell upon that. Instead, she had to focus on finding out all she could about the women and children that were dying on these ships. And it was clear that the brigadier's time in China would be useful to them in their quest.

He was able to stop and converse with people on the street. Some of them clearly wanted nothing to do with the

Englishman. When they saw him approaching, they ran away.

It was not surprising to Sylvia. The brigadier was intimidating in height as well as demeanour. But he was also friendly, and those that did stop and talk with him were rewarded with a shilling from his purse.

After speaking with two or three different people, it became very clear that there were no women in the Limehouse community, at least not young women or children.

The day had been frustrating, and as it would take some time to return to Brighton, the Brigadier suggested that they take rooms at Brown's hotel the night. It was new place in the city, but had an excellent reputation already and Lady Sarah readily agreed.

But her mind was dwelling on the case and she was distracted as they began to make their way out of the Limehouse community.

"What is it your ladyship?" Sylvia asked in a quiet voice, as the Brigadier and the Baker Boys walked ahead of the pair of ladies. Pattinson padded beside them, still unwilling to move from her ladyship's side.

"I had assumed that once we were here, we might find something that would help tell us that women were being brought over to join their husbands to start new lives something of that ilk," Lady Sarah said

"Because they are women and children that would have made sense," Sylvia agreed.

"But there are no women here. There's no other community of Chinese people in London. Why are they coming?" Lady Sarah asked with frustration.

"I fear my lady, that when we find the answer to that question, we will have solved our mystery. But the truths that we learned from it will be far more disturbing than we'd ever wished to know," Sylvia replied.

"I fear you may be right." Lady Sarah says sadly.

"We should not dwell on what we cannot change for now. We will solve this mystery and do what we can for the people involved. And if, as Mr Brown said, there are others that need to be helped and rescued, we can do that too. You cannot change the world all on your own," Silvia smiled.

"Perhaps not. But I can try," Lady Sarah replied with a grin and Sylvia didn't doubt for a second that her employer would do just that.

Chapter
14

Doctor Hales had been a student at the Royal College of Physicians when he was training, and it made a great number of friends there was quite an esteemed and celebrated member of the alumni

He had been back a couple of times since graduating, but never on a matter of such importance and Jack held up some small hope has his colleagues would be able to help. But he was not certain that he would find the answers that he needed. Yet, it was the only place he could think to try.

He walked through the great doors of the college, and down the corridor to where one of his oldest friends, and school friend from his days at the college, Doctor Harold Williams, had his office. Doctor Williams was one of the teachers now at the college, and spent a great deal of time invested in research. But he was also so well connected that anything that happened in the city, he would know about. Jack knocked on the door.

"Enter," Harold's voice boomed from within.

"I know that rather busy men such as yourself, have little time for visiting fellows. But perhaps you could spare me a few moments?" Doctor Hales asked as he opened the door.

"Jack! My God! What brings you here?" Harold said warmly as he stood up from behind his desk and rushed to shake hands with his old friend.

"Unfortunately, nothing good," Jack said with a heavy sigh.

"Well then, please sit and tell me everything," Harold said with a concerned look in his face. It did not take Jack long to explain everything that had happened in the past few days.

"Well, everything that happened down at the beach. I see. Then you think that this might be a wider problem," Harold said when Jack was finished.

"Something like tuberculosis. Yes, I do not see it being an isolated incident," Jack explained.

"No. I think that you are possibly right there," Harold said thoughtfully. "It would make sense after all."

"What is it?" Doctor Hales asked with a frown.

"You say that these women were drowned in the

sea?" Doctor Williams asked.

"Well, they were not drowned at all, but merely their bodies found there," Jack corrected his friend.

"Of course, of course. Makes it very difficult," Harold sighed.

"You've seen other bodies?" Jack frowned.

"Yes," Harold admitted.

"How many?" Doctor Hales asked with interest.

"A few. There are always the drunks that fall in the river at this time of year. That cannot be helped or avoided, it seems. But there have been a large number of women and children especially, female children being found in the water, as of late," Harold said with a frown.

"Is that so?" Jack said with a wry smile, things in his mind beginning to click.

"Yes. I am not really sure what it means if I am honest," Harold shrugged. "It is old that sometimes you get these things happening but what has struck me as rather odd is that nobody seems to want to do anything about it."

"The police are not interested?" Jack asked.

"Why no, not really. They just see it as par for the course," Doctor Williams shrugged.

"I see. and they will be of no help to me," Jack sighed.

"Is there a reason that you're looking so closely into this?" Harold asked.

"Ah, only that it is a dear friend who finds this rather disturbing. She found the bodies, and she cannot leave mysteries alone," Jack said, spreading his hands wide with a helpless expression on his face.

"Ah, a lady," Harold said as though he had solved the mystery all on his own.

"It is not what you might think," Jack corrected his friend.

"No?" Harold asked with a grin.

"No, she is the ward of Brigadier Webb-Kneelingroach. You remember George?" Jack said off-handedly.

"George? Yes, of course. I see, so his ward is the one investigating. Does that mean the brigadier is also involved?" Harold asked.

"It does," Jack said.

"Well, then we have not a moment to lose. Come. I believe there are some bodies down in the morgue that you may want to look at," Harold said and lead the way out of his office and down the stairs to the morgue below.

"You see it is not only women and female children from China that have been turning up dead there have been a few other ethnicities as well. There have been some Indian women and children. Not many granted but a few and some seemingly hail from Africa. I am not sure exactly where, I am not an expert in these things," Harold spoke firmly as they moved quickly. "But it does seem odd that they are all women and female children. It has led to quite the level of discussion, n an academic sense, but none of us have really had the time or the inclination, if I am honest to do any further research into this," Harold said.

"There are so many people in need, so many diseases we cannot possibly be chasing every little thing down," Harold explained.

"Perhaps not," Jack agreed. "But you should know that the bodies I examined, most of the women that were found in Brighton, all of them had extremely advanced tuberculosis."

"I see," Harold said. "Now, that is even more interesting. I shall explain once we have seen the bodies," Harold continued, and the two men walked in silence the rest of the way, each man lost in his own thoughts, as though a great puzzle was about to be solved for them both, and would not of been but for the visit of Doctor Jack Hales to his former school.

Chapter
15

Richard, Oliver, and Alex reached the first ship rather easily, and found most of the crew still at hand.

They tried to question them, but found it quite hard going as not a single one among their number spoke English. It took some time to locate the second ship, but when they did, Alex feared they would meet with the same problem that they had had with the first ship.

He debated whether they should simply give up as it was nearing the two hour mark, when they due to return and meet with Thomas and Edward, and could simply go back, armed with the information that they had the names of two ships that could possibly be involved, and leave the rest to Lady Sarah's imagination or sleuthing skills.

But after it had been Alex and Richard that had obtained the said information, Mr Brown seemed more overzealous about contributing something to their afternoon.

As they were walking over to where the second ship was birthed, Alex noticed a man was following them. He turned to confront the man, and was met with a smiling Chinese face.

"Mayfair says you need interpreter?" the man said. His English was surprisingly good, and his accent was only very slight.

"We do," Richard said cautiously.

"I your man then," he said with all the confidence in the world.

Something about his demeanour,and his willingness to help, made Mr Hunter nervous. There was a general rule that people who wanted money in exchange for information had to often be convinced that you were not wasting their time first. Rather than simply volunteering to help with no reward. This man was stood before them saying that he could help them, without asking for money upfront.

It also struck Richard as strange that a man would try to help them after so many of his countrymen had seemed reticent to even try to understand them. He was all but certain that at least some of the men that they had attempted to speak to on their journey could speak English, at least passively enough to communicate, but just did not want to speak to them about what was going on.

But Mr Brown saw no danger, and was quick to accept the offer of help.

"Yes, we need to we need an interpreter very badly. Come, come, we will pay you handsomely for it as well," Mr Brown said beckoning for the stranger to follow them.

Richard and Alex both exchanged shocked looks as a few moments before they had not been able to convince Mr Brown of the virtues of paying for information, and now here he was willing to pay a small fortune for information that they were not even certain would be any good.

They both tried to stop Oliver, but his hand was in his wallet, and a pile of coins was placed in the smiling man's hands before they knew what was happening.

"Good, good, come with me. I help you find what you need," the man said.

Alexander and Richard exchanged a worried glance, but as Mr Brown had already started to follow the man, they had a little choice but to follow the American to try and keep him out of danger.

The smiling man chatted away the whole time talking about his great love of the Queen, of the British, of all the good things they had done in his homeland - something else that struck Alex as odd.

He knew that Britain had brought a great many changes to China with the introduction of trade there, but he was almost certain that most of the Chinese people had not welcomed the infidels. Especially not as warmly as they were seemingly being led to believe.

It took some time for the man to lead them to a place where he said that they could meet with the captain of the ship and ask him all the questions they wanted.

But as they entered the room there was nobody there, and both Alex and Richard began to think that perhaps they had made a very great mistake in trusting such a man.

Before either of them could back out of the deal that had been made by Mr Brown, everything went dark around the three men the lights in the warehouse had been turned out, and Mr Hunter was certain they would not be leaving the place any time soon.

Chapter
16

The walk back to Brown's Hotel was a quiet one. Lady Sarah was lost in thought, and all four of her companions knew better than to try and speak to her when she was thinking.

As they left the Limehouse community, they found a tea shop with silks in the window just on the edge of the area. Silvia stopped at the window to admire some of the pretty brocade that she saw there.

Lady Sarah noticed an older woman inside the shop. She was standing behind the counter looking desperately worried.

"Perhaps we should stop and take tea, Sylvia. We have barely had a moment today to relax. Brigadier, if you could take the Stanley and Lee to the hotel, and arrange the rooms we will see you there shortly," Lady Sarah said with a smile.

"Of course, of course. We would not want to interrupt tea time between you two ladies," the brigadier smiled, thankful that Lady Sarah seemed to be trying to take her mind off the mystery.

The Baker boys both instantly looked put out that they would be missing tea and cake in the lovely shop that they had just passed. But they made no argument because they were sure the brigadier would spoil them both when Lady Sarah was not looking.

With Patterson at their side, Sylvia and Lady Sarah opened the door to the tea shop and walked in. A couple of tables sat amongst the silks and dresses that hung from the beams. Lady Sarah and Sylvia sat down at one of these tables, and awaited the woman from the counter. She came over presently to take their order.

Growing up in India, Lady Sarah had learned a great deal about tea and the different teas that China offered as well as India. It often meant that she was disappointed with some of the tea that Cooky kept in the kitchen at Grangeback Manor. But over there she had slowly improved the cooks taste in tea, and now there are quite a few different varieties that could be found within the kitchen pantry.

Lapsang Souchong was a particular favourite of Lady Sarah as it had a very strong flavour, one of the strongest flavours that she'd ever experienced in tea, and Sylvia was keen to try it as well. Lady Sarah had spoken of it often, and it was not one that Cooky had ever been able to find at the marketplace. But then again, there wasn't a really strong Chinese community in Cheshire for her to be able to call upon.

The lady nodded as the order was taken, and she seemed quite surprised that an English woman would be ordering such a beverage, but she made no comment and quickly hurried away to fulfil the order. She came back with a number of sweet things that seemed quite exotic and neither woman had had before to accompany their tea.

The contrast between the strong flavour of Lapsang Souchong and the sweet treats was quite delightful, and Silvia almost forgot why it was that they were there.

As the tea was laid out on the table, Lady Sarah reached out, and gently gently touched the hand of the serving woman.

"We know something is happening. We are here to help," Lady Sarah said. The woman looked at her terrified for a moment.

"I know nothing happened. All good, all good," the

woman said.

"No, something is happening. We know," Lady Sarah replied.

"Oh, everything fine," the teashop lady insisted.

"Six women and four children were found at the beach this morning," Lady Sarah said "We know they are not the first we know they will not be the last. Let us help," Lady Sarah said earnestly.

The woman seemed to not know what to say. She looked extremely nervous.

"I cannot say, too dangerous," the woman said.

"Please," Silvia said. "We will do what we can."

The woman looked between Lady Sarah and Sylvia, almost disbelieving of the two women, she sighed and eventually spoke.

"The bad men and women they take good girls from homes. Ones in the country. Ones with no one to miss them. They tell them they will make great money. Be great beauties. Have new lives here. But all lies. They take all money from the girls. Most die. This is not good. It must stop," the woman said. "Please help."

Lady Sarah and Sylvia looked at one another.

"We will do everything we can," Lady Sarah promised. The woman looked like she was satisfied with such a response, and hurried away quickly, not wishing to be seen with the two ladies any further, leaving Lady Sarah and Sylvia to drink their tea in silence, neither of them wishing to say anything else.

The woman returned to her counter, and refused to make eye-contact with the ladies, even when they came to pay. It was clear she felt she was being watched, even in the comfort of her own tea room..

When they had left the shop, Lady Sarah turned to Sylvia and said,

"You are right, the world is a dark and dangerous place."

"My lady?" Sylvia frowned.

"It is nothing, but I fear that we may discover far more dark and dangerous motivations before we are through," Lady Sarah said quietly.

"Will we really be able to help?" Sylvia asked.

"Perhaps, perhaps not, but we will certainly try," Lady Sarah replied.

Chapter
17

Doctor Hales and Doctor Williams decided to examine the bodies together. It had been a long time since either of them had worked together, and both were used to working alone. But the camaraderie that the two had shared in their youth had not been forgotten.

They worked well as a unit, both were possessed of different skills and different disciplines meant they could work more efficiently.

There were eight bodies in total. Jack was surprised that more than two of them were Chinese. Three of them were African and the remaining remaining three were from India.

Each of the bodies, upon receiving a full post mortem, revealed to have the same damage to the head, the same haematoma, and all of the women had tuberculosis.

When they had sewn the bodies backup and cleared away the autopsies, Jack turned to Harold and said,

"You said there was something else interesting that I

should know. Something else that would be helpful?"

"Ah, yes, of course. See, the very interesting thing is that you mentioned the tuberculosis and clearly all of these poor women suffered from it to quite a degree. But there seems to have been a great increase recently, of men with pox coming into the hospitals that are also suffering from tuberculosis," Harold replied.

"Pox and tuberculosis?" Doctor Hales scoffed.

"Yes. It could be nothing, but I thought you should know there is a connection there," Doctor Williams shrugged as he washed his hands.

"Quite," Jack frowned. "How many men, and where in town?"

"Oh, all over. There doesn't seem to be a district that is free of pox," Harold sighed. "But there has been a great increase in brothel activity recently."

"An increase?" Doctor Hales said as he thought on the connection.

"Well, quite," Harold smiled. "But as well that, soldiers have returned from Europe. Wellington's army that fought against Napoleon has all but disbanded. There was no need to keep so many men without a threat to fight. So there has been a great deal of men who are in need of distraction, one might say," Harold said delicately.

"I see, so you believe that these women suffering from tuberculosis are perhaps?" Doctor Hales replied and let the question hang in the air, unfinished.

"Yes, ladies of the night, it would seem, though I can't say for certain of course," Harold said with a shrug. "But one can draw conclusions from such an increase in pox and tuberculosis."

"Yes, one can," Jack said thoughtfully.

"What is it my friend?" Doctor Williams asked.

"I have been friends with the brigadier's ward for quite some time. She's a sweet girl. Very charming. Very clever. She wants to see the best in humanity. I fear that all she shall learn from this is how terrible humans can really be to one another," Doctor Hales sighed sadly.

"We cannot protect people from the evils of the world forever," Dr. Williams replied simply.

"No, indeed. But we can wish that we could. Surely," Doctor Hales replied.

"Ah, if wishes were horses, beggars would ride," Doctor Williams said clapping his friend on the shoulder.

"You are quite right of course, quite right," Jack sighed heavily. "Thank you for your help today, Harold. I appreciate it more than you know."

"Of course, of course. Will you be in town long? You must come have dinner with Elena and I," Harold said "It be most welcome."

"I would be glad to see her again. It has been too long," Doctor Hales accepted the invitation.

"And you must tell me of how Richard and Gordon fare. Are they both still planning on being doctors?" Harold asked.

"Richard, yes, he is part of my practice. But for the moment, he has taken some time off as there has been some unpleasantness as of late," Jack said, and paused.

"And what of Gordon?" Harold insisted on knowing.

"Gordon is gone to America," Jack said hurriedly.

"I see. Part of the unpleasantness?" Harold asked with a sympathetic look on his face.

"Yes, but it is a long story," Jack sighed.

"Well, come tell us over dinner this evening. I am sure that Elena will be thrilled to see you," Harold said jovially, lightening the mood.

"Very well, dinner it is," Jack agreed with a smile. "But only dinner. I shall not impose upon our hospitality all night."

"Come now, old friend, you must take a bed with us for the night. What a poor host I should be!" Harold exclaimed.

"No, I shall take rooms at Brown's Hotel for the night," Jack said politely.

"Oh, you must stay with us, please. I insist," Harold said firmly.

"No, my dear friend I cannot impose. Dinner is more than enough. I will have to start early to head back to Brighton with news of my discoveries. My friends cannot wait forever," Jack said with a smile.

"Oh well. Then we shall enjoy you while we can," Harold said with a smile.

"That is all any of us can do, surely?" Jack replied with a grin.

"Now that is the man that I knew of old. Always quick with a joke and a smile," Harold said warmly.

"We shall be merry this evening, though not too late. I do have to get up early," Jack laughed.

"Yes, our days of carefree abandon are long behind us now," Harold sighed with a deep longing for the past.

"Agreed," Jack said with a wisp of nostalgia

"To be young again," Harold replied with a hefty sigh.

Chapter
18

Lee and Stanley Baker did not quite know what to expect from Brown's Hotel. The name was much talked of, but they had no real understanding of what it meant until they saw the hotel.

They had seen many grand things in their lives, and they were certain that they would see many more grand things in the days to come, but nothing quite prepared them for the grandness of Brown's Hotel. It was beautiful and elegant, from the moment that they stepped through the doors, and the pair quite feared that they would be turned out on their ears for not looking as sophisticated as the rest of the clientèle.

When the brigadier gave his name at the desk to the concierge, who had looked at the two boys with arched eyebrows, had a complete shift in demeanour.

A moment or two later, the manager appeared as if from nowhere and was greeting the brigadier as an old friend. George introduced the Baker Boys and they too, were greeted most warmly.

Rooms were arranged and the two boys were each given their own, something that they never had in their had before in their lives. Even when staying at the manor house, the boys had shared a bedroom. It was not out of spirit of meanness that Mrs Bosworth had put the two boys in the same room, but more so that they would not feel so alone and isolated in the manor house when they had first come to stay there.

When they had eventually moved into their own bedrooms, it had been something of a revelation to the two boys, but having their own bedrooms was something quite different to simply having their own hotel room.

The boys had bother thanked the brigadier profusely before exploring their rooms. Sylvia and Lady Sarah also had separate rooms arranged from them, right across the hall from where the brigadier and the Baker Boys rooms lay.

It did not take long for Lady Sarah and Sylvia to catch up to the party, and they were quite pleased with the arrangements that had been made.

Dinner that evening was held in the restaurant, something that Lee and Stanley Baker had also not known quite what to expect. But they had been overwhelmed by the quality of the food and the respect with which they were treated by the serving staff.

There was something quite amazing about the whole experience. It was certainly something that they were sure would never again be repeated in their lives. At least not outside the company of the brigadier and Lady Sarah.

It was late in the evening and the Baker Boys had been sent off to bed, when the brigadier spotted Doctor Hales checking in to the hotel.

"Why Jack, fancy seeing you here!" the brigadier said loudly enough to make the heads of other guests in the lobby turn.

"I see, you are here as well. So much for allowing me to examine the bodies before investigating," Doctor Hales grinned.

"You know we always like to be on top of things," the brigadier said with a grin.

"I doubt very much that it was you who began the investigation," Jack said sternly.

Lady Sarah flashed a knowing smile at the doctor.

"You must have discovered a great many things

during your day of investigation. I know I have," the doctor said.

"Yes, you must sit down and we shall share all we can about what we have discovered," Lady Sarah said brightly.

Doctor Hales agreed and the brigadier went in search of a waiter to secure some brandy for the two men.

Lady Sarah and Sylvia did not partake, but sat at a small table in the furthest corner of the bar where they could be discreet in their conversations, and not easily overheard.

Doctor Hales explained about the tuberculosis and about the women from other nations besides China, as well as the increasing number of men with pox and tuberculosis turning up.

Lady Sarah spoke of the additional bodies that had been found in Brighton, of the port close by to the beach, and the information the Chinese woman in the tea shop had provided.

When all had been spoken of and shared, the group collapsed into a nice uneasy silence.

"It does not point to anything good," Doctor Hales said sadly when he could not longer bear the silence.

"No, but I cannot understand what it would be," Lady

Sarah said. "Now that slavery is illegal. There are so few with any real money who would engage in it, and that is all I can think of," she said with a deep sigh.

"Come, let it not trouble you too much. For this evening, let us rest. We will need to set off early tomorrow morning too return to Brighton," the brigadier said

"Yes, you're quite right, George, of course. We should rest well. You never know, a little sleep, and we could wake up and know the answer to it all," the doctor said, looking at Lady Sarah in an effort to comfort her.

Sylvia shifted uncomfortably as an idea had floated to her mind that she did not voice aloud. It did not seem possible that there would be no connection between the dead women and the poxed men.

But it seemed that her friends were all searching for a reason that the women would be killed. Not the reason the women were being brought there in the first place.

Sylvia had a sinking feeling that she knew exactly why the women were being ripped from their homes, why it was only girls, and that though, they may end the suffering and a great injustice for a small group of women, by solving this case there would be no way for them to end up practice entirely.

Sylvia was the last to leave the bar. She had no drink to finish but her thoughts had turned to how dark the evil motivations of the human spirit could be, and she did not wish to sleep until she could find one sliver of hope in humanity to cling on to.

"Sylvia, are you not going to bed?" Lady Sarah asked as she reappeared in the bar.

"Yes, I am," Sylvia said, masking the doubts she had with a smile.

"Things always look better in the morning," Lady Sarah gave her a half smile.

"Perhaps, but for tonight, I would like to find a reason to believe in the goodness of people," Sylvia sighed and shook her head.

"Then remember this, you are a reason to believe in the goodness of people. You have done so much for me, the Baker boys and even the brigadier. Hold onto your own heart and know that you are a bright light in whatever darkness comes," Lady Sarah said without hesitation.

Sylvia looked up at her employer and smiled.

"It will do," she replied and the two women made

their way to their rooms to rest for the night.

Chapter
19

Richard opened his eyes and felt immediately sick to his stomach. He was dizzy and could not think of where he was or how he got there. He also had no explanation as to why he was sick or why he could not move his hands or legs.

Wherever he was, it was dark. But he was sure he was not alone. A groan next to him told him that, at the very least, Mr Brown was with him.

"Are you quite well?" Richard asked.

"No, no, I am not," Mr Brown growled.

"I see, can you move?" Richard asked. Sounds of struggling and shuffling answered Richard's question long before Mr Brown did.

"It seems I cannot," Oliver sighed

"No, I cannot either," Richard replied.

"Does your head feel as though it has been stuck in a bell and rung?" Alexander's voice interrupted their conversation.

"Indeed it does," Mr Brown confirmed.

"At least we are not alone. Do you know where we are?" Richard said, sounding the slightest bit hopeful.

"That I do not know," Mr Hunter sighed. "You have both been asleep for a few hours more than I. In that time. I have learned nothing, at least nothing useful at any rate."

"Mr Hunter, you say you have learned nothing useful," Richard said. "Does that meant that you have learned something you do not consider useful?"

"Well, I know that we have not left the shipyard, and I can still smell the sea. When you listen very carefully, you can hear them at work in the shipyard. Other than that, I'm also at a loss," Mr Hunter shrugged, or at least tried to, but found when he tried to move his shoulders that pain seared through them.

"Then we have been captured," Richard said flatly

"So it would seem. But by whom and for what purpose?" Mr Brown asked.

"I suspect that our smiling friend his behind it," Mr Hunter replied dryly.

"He did seem too eager to help," Richard agreed.

"Come now, how is that any different from the man Mayfair? You are jumping to conclusions," Mr Brown insisted.

"I do not think so," Mr. Hunter said shortly. The men lapsed into an uncomfortable silence which was only broken when the door, to wherever they were being held, creaked open.

"Your friend is right. Never trust a smiling man. The smile always hide something," a voice that was familiar announced and was accompanied by footsteps entering the room.

"Then why play the smiling man?" Mr Hunter asked. He recognised the voice as once as belonging to the man who had approached them.

His English had greatly improved in a short space of time, and Mr Brown felt exceedingly foolish.

"Because though you should never trust a smiling man. There are always those that do," the man replied.

"And for what reason are you holding us here?" Richard asked, trying to sound confident in the face of unknown circumstances.

"Well, surely that must be obvious, even to you gentleman," the man said curtly.

"Quite," Mr Hunter reply dryly.

"You will tell us all that you know, all that we wish to hear from you, and perhaps one day you will be allowed to see England again," the smiling man said, as though it was an explanation.

Mr Hunter bit his tongue to stop himself from saying something he would regret. Richard was at a loss for words, and Oliver was confused.

"Sir, I am an American," Mr Brown said trying to gather his thoughts.

"Then, you should have known not to interfere. The British no do not know any better, but you, you Americans have your independence now. Do you not wish to be free of subjugation and interference? So, why is it that you have engaged in such here?" the smiling man asked.

Mr Brown had no answer for him, and rather than risk upsetting the man he held his tongue.

"Now, now, come gentlemen. Staying silent will not help you here," the smiling man said. "We are all friends, surely. But if you wish, we can do this the hard way. I will ask you some questions, and if I do not get the answers I want, or any answers at all, then my associates will ensure that you will answer," the smiling man explained.

Light was now being cast into the room, and though the men could make out vague shapes, they could not make out any faces clearly.

Mr Brown had never been in this situation before and neither had Mr Hales, but Mr Hunter had dealt with men like this many times. He knew that the moment that the questioning was over, the moment that they were of no more use to the smiling man, they would find themselves executed and buried in unmarked graves with no one to ever know what had happened to them.

To answer the questions would lead to death. Not answering the questions would also end in the same way. So all that they could do was play for time, and hope that Thomas and Edward had evaded capture and had the good sense to summon help before searching for them.

Chapter
20

The party checked out of the hotel early, leaving plenty of time to return from London. They had hoped to be back at White House before breakfast, but as they returned, they found the house in uproar.

Edward was comforting Mary and Charlotte, who were beside themselves with grief. Thomas was preparing to set out to London in search of the group when the carriage pulled up at the house.

"What is it? What is wrong?" the brigadier asked as he stepped out of the carriage towards the waiting Mr Egerton.

"Mr Hunter, Mr Brown, and Mr Hales did not return," Thomas reported solemnly.

"What the devil do you mean, did not return?" the brigadier asked gruffly.

"When we were exploring the shipyards, we split into two groups. Edward and I we went to explore the shipbuilding area for any information we could find, and the other three they went in search of ships that the women and children could have come from. We agreed that we would spend two hours looking, and then we would meet back where we started. They never returned to meet with us. We waited three hours. We called on the local constabulary and no sign of them has been found," Thomas replied.

"This is grave news, indeed," Doctor Hales said grimly. Lady Sarah could not speak. She had been so tired of the two men and bickering over her, she simply wanted them to be far away, and now they were missing. She feared that she might never see either of them again.

"It is not your fault," Sylvia hissed under her breath to her mistress.

"Then whose fault is it?" Lady Sarah whispered in reply.

"Whoever has captured them," Sylvia said. Lady Sarah knew that Sylvia was not wrong. But it did not mean that she did not feel responsible for their disappearance.

"Then to the dockyards at once we go," the brigadier said.

"Edward must remain here with the ladies," Thomas said.

"One quite understands," Brigadier George replied

without a trace of ill-feeling. He was focused on finding his son and the other two missing men.

Horses were changed for the carriage before they set out. The second carriage had already been readied to go in search of them.

Sylvia and the Baker Boys elected to wait for the horses on the carriage to be changed so that Thomas, the brigadier, Pattinson, Doctor Hales and Lady Sarah might go ahead of them in the carriage that had already been prepared.

Nobody spoke as the coach lurched forwards, bound for Shoreham-by-Sea.

Doctor Hales wished that he's allowed his son to come with him now to take part in the autopsies. Lady Sarah still held onto regret about how harshly she had spoken to both men.

The brigadier was worried that he would lose his son before he could recognise him at court. Thomas fretted over the fate of his cousin. Pattinson was sat in the middle of the floor of the carriage, turning to each of the passengers in turn to lick each of their hands, trying to comfort them.

He knew that something was wrong, but he had no way of comprehending what had happened, only the stress that each of his companions exuded. Although the act was appreciated there was nothing the dog could do to make anything any better.

When they arrived at the dock yard, it was clear that Scotland Yard had finally been mobilised to search for the young men.

They did not appreciate the presence of civilians who would interfere in their investigations.

"That is my son that is missing. Damn it," the brigadier yelled when a pimply looking constable tried to turn them away.

"And we will find him in time, sir, I am sure," the constable said, not knowing how close he was to a broken nose. But rather than hitting the constable, the brigadier had another idea.

He stood in the middle of the shipyard and raised his normally booming voice to an even greater volume, so that it might be heard above the clattering and banging of the shipyard.

"Three men are missing from this port. They were last seen yesterday, and there was a reward for anyone - anyone at all - that can give us information that will let us find them," he cried out and every head turned towards him. Work in the shipyard had ceased in the wake of the announcement.

"What kind of reward?" one of the labourers asked.

"Twice what you make in a year," the brigadier called back. Such a princely reward sent rumblings amongst all of the workers in the yard who laid down their tools and came over to see how they could help in the search.

"Now, now, now, we do not need everyone to help in order to find these men," the constable tried to disperse the crowd. But since the brigadier had made such a kingly offer as a reward, the constable's words fell on deaf ears.

"Three fellows? Yes?" One very tall?" one of the men asked.

"That is right," the brigadier confirmed.

"One of them was American. The other well-spoken but without arrogance?" the man continued.

"That is quite correct," Doctor Hales said as he looked at man volunteering the information with suspicion.

"I saw them. I spoke to them even. My name is Mayfair. They paid me several guineas for some information," Mayfair replied.

"And what was the information?" Lady Sarah asked.

"They wanted to know about these Chinese ships, you see. I told them what I knew. They went off to find them, I guess," Mayfair said.

"I see that is extremely helpful. Do you know which ships they were?" Thomas asked.

"That I do, sir. And I will even take you to see them myself," Mayfair offered.

There were some British sailors leaning against a wall wall nearby watching the exchange between Mayfair and the group.

"Why do you want to know all this?" one of them asked.

"One of the missing men is my son," the brigadier said. "Another is the doctor's son, and the other is the cousin of this fine gentleman."

"Is that all?" another of the British sailors asked.

"No, sir, it is not," Lady Sarah said as she stepped forward. "They came on my instruction. You see we are looking to solve the mystery of how the bodies of women and children came to be floating in the sea of Brighton. A great deal of lives have been lost, and we wished to stop whatever was causing this. But now our friends are missing, and there could be more women in danger as well as our friends we do not know until we find them," Lady Sarah said honestly.

"Well, boys, it is good enough for me. Round up the lads," the sailor who was clearly in charge of the group said.

"Sir?" Lady Sarah asked with a frown.

"Oh, we can not very well leave women and children in danger or your friends. Will take us a few minutes to gather up all the lads but then we'll help you search wherever you need to. And we will not be taking your reward, sir," the sailor replied. Mayfair blushed, but he still had no intention of giving up the reward.

"I am most grateful to you," the doctor said

"We have some other friends who are not far behind us," Thomas said. "A woman and two boys. Would someone be good enough to bring them to us when they arrive?"

"I will leave Pete here ,"the sailor said. "He is a bit long in the tooth for going on a great adventure, but he is a damn good look out and will be able to bring your friends along no problem."

Lady Sarah nodded her thanks and the sailor fairly blushed. Despite his embarrassment, he was true to his word. Over one hundred men seem to assemble, as if from nowhere, in order to help them search and not one of them would take any of the brigadier's money for doing so.

News of why they were in the dockyard in the first place had spread quickly, and just as it had a disgusted Lady Sarah that women and children should be treated such a way, the sailors were equally appalled.

Their reaction had surprised Lady Sarah, and she was sure that Silvia would be equally surprised when she finally arrived.

Mayfair was as good as his word as well. He lead the group across the far side of the docks where the two ships lay at anchor, but he took his reward, and soon vanished, his part in the great search over.

Lady Sarah was glad to see him go. There was something about the man that she did not like nor trust. But she had no time to think on what it could be about Mayfair that she did not like.

Her main concern now was finding out what had happened to her friends ,and rescuing them as soon as she possibly could.

Chapter
21

Constable Arwyn Evans had been quite reticent about Constable Buckley joining him in Stickleback Hollow. It was not due to any grudge or slight against the man personally, but experience had shown that those assigned to Stickleback Hollow, as of late, had not been the best choices for policing the village.

In fact, it was safe to say, they were examples of the worst kind of policeman. But he was ready to give Constable Buckley a chance; ready to be proven wrong and have the line of terrible constable end.

Arwyn decided that in order to teach Thompson Buckley about Stickleback Hollow the best thing would be to walk about the village, and allow the constable to get to know the place and understand the people there more readily.

The residents of Stickleback Hollow were certainly a unique group of people, and Constable Evans was determined to introduce Thompson to as many people as possible on the first day he was in the village, but a cursory introduction to people was hardly getting to know them.

Constable Evans liked to walk around the village every day, and talk with people. Talking with them is how he built respect and a rapport with the village inhabitants.

Which meant when they were in trouble, they were able to come and talk with him. It also allowed him to see if there were new faces in the village, or discover quickly if anything unusual had happened. Unusual events were often connected to one another, especially in a place as small as Stickleback Hollow..

Constable Buckley was not sure quite what to expect when he had been assigned to the village. He had heard many rumours about the place, and the people there, but he was sure that it was all exaggerated.

Now that he was in Stickleback Hollow, he could see that if anything, the stories had been under exaggerated. He found Wilson's Inn to be charming, Wilson, the barkeeper and owner, to be a rather companionable sort, and his wife's cooking was second to none

He enjoyed speaking with Mr Pick, the greengrocer, with Mr. Christian, about all of his adventures as a missionary, though he did find that the Reverend Percy

Butterfield was a little bit dry and long winded on the subject of trains.

In his discussions with the people, he found a varied range of opinions on many things, from the best way to grow roses, to who should have won the best vegetable award at the latest summer fete. What surprised him more than anything else was not the fanatical love of cricket this village seemed to have, but the time and effort that every villager seemed to be putting into preparing for the wedding of Miss Beaumont and Mr Claydon.

Angela Baker was hard at work, creating a wedding dress for Miss Beaumont and Mr Claydon's suit. The seamstress had had two girls from the village to help her, as her sons were away with Lady Sarah. Her progress was slow, but by all reports, the gowns and other wedding outfits would be ready well before the big day arrived.

Emma and several of the women were helping to create the wedding feast. They had made a great deal of notes on what needed to be done, as ordinarily it would have been Cooky from Grangeback Manor in charge of these preparations.

Cooky had made a great list of all that needed to be

done for the wedding, and left it in the capable hands of women that she trusted to do a good job. She would be back, no doubt, in plenty of time to oversee all the cooking on the day, but there were ingredients to be bought, and recipes to be tested - especially as Mr Claydon had requested some delicacies that he had fallen in love with in his time as an explorer.

The Reverend Butterfield was busy crafting the perfect marriage service, with the help of Mr Clayton and Miss Beaumont to guide him in their tastes. The organist was practising night and day to ensure that she would give the best possible performance.

Every person in the village, it did not matter their profession, their standing, or how long they had lived there were all involved. Even Constable Evans had been given a list of tasks that he had to complete.

"What is it they have you doing?" the new constable asked after they had been walking the village for a short time.

"I am in charge of cleaning all the seating that will be used at the manor," Constable Evans said with a measure of disappointment.

"I see," Thompson said sounding quite surprised at

the task.

"We all have to do our bit," Arwyn shrugged.

"It is a bit odd, though, do you not think?" Constable Buckley asked.

"What do you mean?" Arwyn asked.

"Well, everyone has been involved in this. It is a little bit unusual, You have to admit," Thompson said slowly.

"This is not what you expected?" Arwyn smiled

" Not at all," Constable Buckley agreed.

"Stickleback Hollow is unusual place. There is a lot that goes on here that you might not expect. But though it is unexpected, it is also quite wonderful at the same time," Arwyn said kindly.

"You're not from here, then?" Constable Buckley asked.

"No. Do I sound like I am?" Arwyn teased him

"I did not like to say anything, but no," Thompson admitted.

"I have lived here long enough now that I would definitely call it home," Arwyn said. "It did feel unusual when I first arrived as well. The village is filled with good people though," He assured the constable.

"But everybody has been so eager to tell me about my predecessors and how they behaved here," the constable complained.

"Oh, you've heard the stories? Then can you blame them? Arwyn asked.

"I guess not," Comfortable agreed eventually. "It is rather strange that you would have so many constables that proved to be so detrimental to so many."

"Indeed," Constable Evans agreed. "But I am sure we have broken that pattern now with you, or at least I hope so. I would be most upset to find that you are just like the ones we've had before."

"I will do my best not to be a disappointment," Constable Buckley smiled.

Chapter
22

The questioning went on for hours. Richard wasn't even sure how long they had been there now. It felt like weeks, at least two, perhaps three. The pain that had been inflicted made it impossible to gauge time.

The torture methods they used had been exceedingly effective and extremely unwelcome. But none had been effective enough to convince the men that they needed to share any information with their captors.

In fact, their incarceration had done nothing to loosen their tongues, and everything to tighten them

Mr Hunter had been the most adamant they knew nothing that would help that captors, and Richard knew that if it had not been for Alex's resolute lies, Richard, at least, would have broken long ago. He could not speak for Mr Brown, but the son of the doctor expected the same was true for him. As much as he would be loath to admit that he owed any debt to Mr Hunter.

They did not know how long they should expect the

torture to continue, but Richard was certain that unless they were rescued, no one would ever know what had happened to them.

He hoped that by failing to meet Thomas and Edward, they had sent for help immediately, but he also wondered whether Thomas and Edward had met a similar fate, and if so, then no one would be coming to help them.

He kept his fears to himself. Not that he would have been able to share them with his friends now that they were being tortured so mercilessly, but he also did not want to appear weak before their captors.

Richard knew that he'd lost consciousness more than once, but did not know whether or not his friends had done the same. In his mind he was holding on to the hope that things would soon be over, one way or another

He had been listening to the sounds of the world outside trying to focus on those instead of what the pain of is wounds. He found the longer that he could listen to the voices outside, the less it bothered him that he was where he was. Sounds outside gave him hope. Hope he would once again be outside and this ordeal would be over.

He had noticed that there had been a great increase in

the sound of voices on the deck above in the past few minutes. Confirmation to him that he was on a ship, and they were somewhere in the hold. He wasn't exactly sure where, it was the first time he had ever been on a ship. But he could tell they were nowhere close to the surface from the sounds of the water lapping against the metal, being so close at hand, and the distance the voices sounded from him.

He had not thought the increase in voices to be strange at first, it was just noise in a foreign language he could not understand. But there was now an urgency to each of those voices, and he even began to think that he recognised some of the sounds that they sounded almost English.

In fact he was certain that they sounded as though they were English. He closed his eyes and focused, blocking out his pain to listen to what was being said.

Shouts, calls, he even thought he heard his own name being shouted.

There it was again.

Now he was certain that his name was being shouted from above.

The smiling Chinese man, who had been in charge of torturing them, was no longer smiling.He looked quite worried, and then there was the rushing sound of feet on deck. People clamouring to be elsewhere. Then light like flooded into the room, causing his eyes to sting and he closed them tight against it.

"They are in here!" a familiar voice sounded, and the next thing he felt strong and familiar arms wrapped around him. "My boy never do this to me again," his father whispered in his ear with relief.

Richard thought he was going to cry, hearing the sounds of his father's voice. The next thing he felt was a soft hand untying the ropes around his wrists, and he could hear Lady Sarah apologising profusely.

He was not sure when exactly he had started crying, but he felt no shame in it for help had finally come.

Sylvia and the Baker Boys had been a full half hour behind them and had joined the group just before they began to explore the ship.

Pattinson was barking and that was gratefully bounding around now that their friends had been found.

But no one seemed to be paying too much attention to the smiling man, who tried to slip away from the ship. But he did not avoid the watchful gazes of Lee and Stanley Baker, who gave chase. Seeing the two boys running after a man, Patterson joined in gleefully and brought the smiling man down with avengeance.

Mr Hunter had weakly identified him, so the police carried him off the questioning. But none of the men were in much condition to provide any more information about who the man was or what he had wanted from them. Doctor Hales had insisted that any questions be held until the men were feeling better.

The sailors had all been thanked for their help, and though they all tried to reject any reward, Lady Sarah had insisted, and it was not in the power of any of the sailors to deny the desires of a lady.

The doctor had overseen the removal of Mr Hunter, Mr Hales and Mr Brown from the ship and the loading of the men into the carriages. When had been ferried back to the White House in Brighton, Doctor Hales had put all three men to bed, ensuring that each of them was going to rest well with as little interference as possible from anyone else. Especially the housekeeper.

Relief was rife in the household. The brigadier and Doctor Hales shared a drink in celebration. Lady Sarah had merely done her best not to break down into a full flood of tears.

The doctor had told her not to worry, an that he would ensure that all three men returns to health as quickly as possible. But Lady Sarah could not help but wonder what the three men had been enduring at the hands of their Chinese captors.

She did not question the good doctor or his expertise, but simply hoped that he was right. There was little she could do at the White House, other than fret and worry. So rather than wait around the house, she decided that she would be of more use of returning to London to speak with the police at Scotland Yard as to what had been discovered from the smiling man.

Lee and Stanley, as well as Pattinson, decided to accompany her, the four of them leaving the others behind, though when the brigadier had discovered that the four had set off, he and Sylvia with Thomas and Edward were not too far behind.

There had been little that the police had been able to share with them, and Scotland Yard would not tell them anything of what the smiling man's involvement was, or what he had been trying to learn from their three friends.

Lady Sarah soon gave up speaking with the constables that were trying to prevent her from interfering, so she and the Baker boys returned to Brown's Hotel intending to stay the night before returning to Brighton. It had been a long day and they were all tired, and she did not want to subject them to yet another tiring journey before they had a chance to rest properly.

But as they entered the hotel, Lady Sarah noticed someone who did not belong there. A very well dressed woman doing her best to hide her face and her features behind a long veil and hat.

Lady Sarah could see that the woman was Chinese in an instant. The hat and veil drawing more attention than they were avoiding. She found it odd that such a woman would be in such a place, not for lack of wealth, but that a woman trying to hide her identity so much, would be in such a public place.

The woman was just leaving the lobby, making her way out into the night, and rather than checking at the hotel Lady Sarah decided to follow her and see where she went.

The brigadier had already checked in to Brown's

Hotel. He had been waiting in the lobby for them to appear, and when he spied his ward, the Baker Boys and Pattinson departing quickly he became quite anxious as to what was happening.

He trusted that his ward would know enough to keep herself out of danger, or at least have the forethought of mind to send the Baker Boys for help as soon as she could. At the very least Pattinson would protect her.

Lady Sarah and the Baker boys followed the woman through the streets of London, not sure what they were expecting to find, or where she might lead them.

But it became increasingly clear as they walked, that she was not a prostitute bound for a brothel. She was not a fallen woman, something that Lady Sarah had suspected from the moment she had laid eyes on the woman.

They followed her for a great deal of time, further than the Lee and Stanley had expected.

Eventually, the woman led them to a warehouse. It stood close to a disused dock and looked to have seem far better days. Th veiled woman opened the door and slipped inside after she had confidently approached the building.

Lady Sarah waited for a few moments before

following cautiously behind her, with Lee and Stanley close at her side. Pattinson was crawling along the floor to avoid detection.

At the end they entered the warehouse, they could see that it was full of boxes and crates, all of which appeared to be empty. And that was not the only thing that was in this warehouse. At the far end of the room was a cell that was filled with women and children, all of whom were covered in grime, dirt and muck. Some were coughing. Others were crying.

It was the most horrific sight that Lady Sarah had ever set her eyes on.

She did not know what to make of the scene before her. But she knew that she was finally close to finding the answer she had been seeking

Chapter
23

"Go back, and fetch the brigadier at once," Lady Sarah said in a hushed voice.

"He is all the way in Brighton," Lee replied.

Of course he is not. He's already at Brown's Hotel. I saw him in the lobby. He and Sylvia followed us here with Thomas and Edward. Bring all of them. We have little time," Lady Sarah instructed.

Neither Lee or Stanley were happy about leaving her ladyship behind, but they nodded their agreement as they knew that as long as Pattinson was with her, she would be safe. The Akita was worth ten men in a fight.

Lady Sarah knew that by sending the Baker Boys to fetch help, she would be leaving herself vulnerable, but she was certain that the Brigadier would be quick to return with the boys. And she hoped that when he did, he would also have the foresight to bring the police with him as well.

Lady Sarah did her best to stay low and hidden, and listened to whatever she could, to try and discover what exactly was happening. Finding the women and children was just the first part of the mystery, the rest of it would be discovering why they were there at all.

The well-dressed woman seemed to be waiting for someone and Lady Sarah realised that if she stayed where she was, when this person entered, she would soon be discovered.

She and Patterson quickly moved, dodging between crates to stay out of sight, to try and get away from the door, and still be in a position where they could see and hear everything.

The labyrinth of boxes made it easy in some respects. But Lady Sarah was also aware that if they moved too much, they would attract unwanted attention and soon be discovered.

She waited in silence, her hand on the collar of Pattinson to keep him quite, until the door opened. Three men walked in and over to where the Chinese woman waited.

"Gentlemen," she said in a silken voice. "So nice of you to join us. I have exactly what you're looking for."

Lady Sarah did not know who these three men were, but judging from their clothing they were wealthy men but not gentleman.

"And what exactly is it that you have for us?" one of the men asked.

"Girls, young and even younger. To help restock your brothels after we have had so many issues with our product," the woman said.

"It has not been easy getting rid of them one of them," one of the other men said with frustration. "It used to be you could dump a body in the streets, and now what a bother is it. There is a new police force, they are starting to make take notice, and ask questions. Why we could not just keep the Bow Street Runners," he grumbled.

"While we have endeavoured to solve this issue at the source, any women or girls that are showing signs of the disease are being dealt with before they even arrive in the country," the woman said. Lady Sarah felt sick to her stomach to hear the woman talk of human lives in such a way.

To be discussing this with brothel owners made it clear to Lady Sarah, that the woman and girls were being trapped into prostitution, not understanding what lives that they were selling themselves into.

"Do you think that will be enough?" the third man

asked.

"Oh, it should be quite enough," the woman replied. "After all, if the sick ones are taken out before they infect the rest then there can be no illness, and no problems. It means that you and I can go on to have a very long and profitable business relationship."

"What is all this we hear about a raid on the shipping docks in Shoreham? Is that not where you are bringing the girls in through?" the first man demanded.

"I can assure you that whatever was happening on those docks has nothing to do with our business arrangements whatsoever," the woman said confidently, but Lady Sarah noticed that a shift in her body language gave away that the line of questions made her nervous.

"All right, then we will talk price," the second man said and the three men went to sit down at a table. But before they could begin their negotiations, the door to the warehouse was kicked open and policemen alongside the brigadier began to rush in. Lady Sarah breathed a sigh of relief as the three men and the woman were all apprehended.

The woman tried to protest in broken English, feigning ignorance, claiming that she was one of the victims and had nothing to do with the brothel owners. But Lady Sarah stood up from where she'd been hiding and announced that all to be lies.

At the sound of the voice of her voice, the Chinese woman turned nasty. she shrieked at Lady Sarah in her native language. The brigadier laughed and replied to carry out such threats as those, the woman would have to pick another target.

"You will not get close enough to harm this girl."

The police were quick to ferry the brothel owners to Scotland Yard, where a representative from the foreign office was also waiting. The interrogation did not last very long before the police were sent out again to round up others that have been implicated by the brothel owners. The Foreign Office have taken charge of the women that they found in their warehouse. The women had been cleaned up, given food, and warm clothing, and were promised to be returned to their home country as soon as possible.

Those at the Foreign Office were shocked to have discovered such a thing going on under their very noses. Lady Sarah refrained from commenting that they'd seem to be quite disinterested when the brigadier had called on them for help; when Scotland Yard had been pressed to assist them earlier too. She was just glad that these women were safe for now.

The brigadier, Lady Sarah, and Pattinson returned to Brown's Hotel in order to rest before travelling back down to Brighton. They had to report to their friends the good news that the case had finally been solved.

Chapter
24

Lady Sarah decided to call upon Commissioner Jonnes-Smith at her earliest convenience. It had been two days since the incident at the warehouse, and a great deal of men had been arrested, as well as some women, who were all involved in the operation.

Lady Sarah had been back to the tea room where the old woman had worked to find that it had been abandoned. She wondered about the old woman's involvement in the operation, and decided that she had to flee, rather than face those who were now being tracked by the police and the Foreign Office.

There was something about it all that still did not sit well with her ladyship. But at least, for now, it was all at an end.

Commissioner Jonnes-Smith was only too happy to see the lady again. He invited her into his office and the two sat and talked for a while about nothing. They both knew that what Lady Sarah would have to say was not a pleasant conversation to be had and it was a natural to hold a pleasant conversation until Lady Sarah changed the subject.

She told the commissioner of everything that they had discovered, the actions that they had taken in the course of their investigation, of everything she had seen at the warehouse and heard, and finally, all the police in the foreign office were now doing.

The commissioner listened with a grave look on his face, and nodded sagely at the appropriate moments. When she had finished, the commission stood and went to look out the window at the spread of Brighton that lay before for him.

"It is easy to think that all men and all women have good in their hearts, but those people who do, they do not know what we do. Good is something that must be protected. Just as we must fight against and evil, grapple with it every opportunity. I will not preach to you, you do not need me to speak to you about those poor souls out there that give into the darkness. I cannot feel anything but pity for them. Pity that they have fallen to such dark ways. Knowing what I know I shall keep watch, do all I can to prevent this happening again and I shall speak to the other Commissioners. We have the other leaders of our church to ensure that we shall be ready for whenever these villains resurface," he said some soberly.

"Then you think they will resurface?" Lady Sarah asked.

"We both know that is inevitable that they will. Money is at stake. People are willing to do the most dastardly things to their fellow man in order to obtain it. Lust of the flesh, especially young flesh is a depraved practice, but it's one that I fear shall only increase as time goes by. But we shall do all we can to stem the flow. You have done a great service to those women in our country, and to our God," the commission said.

"In truth, I did not have any of that in mind when I set out to solve this case. I merely saw a mystery that needed to be solved," Lady Sarah admitted.

"I do not believe that is true," the commissioner said. "I believe your compassion and heart, your love for people is what drives you to solve these mysteries. You set the scales of justice in balance to ensure that victims do not go unheard, no matter where they might be from. No, you do yourself a great discredit," the commissioner said thoughtfully. "How long will you stay in Brighton?" he asked, changing the subject.

"Another few days, our friends still have to recover somewhat from their ordeal," Lady Sarah admitted.

"Well, Brighton is the best place for it. The sea has wonderful healing properties," the commissioner smiled. "Perhaps I shall come and meet them, or maybe you would all come see us on Sunday." the commissioner said

"Perhaps we shall," Lady Sarah agreed. "But for now I have taken up enough of your time, sir. It has been a pleasure to meet you."

"The pleasure really has been all mine. I look forward to hearing of all the great things you will do in the future. All those lives you will save, all those rights wrongs you will right," the commissioner said, turning away from the window.

"Perhaps," Lady Sarah replied. "But one person cannot change the world."

"Oh, I do not think that is true. I think one person can change many worlds. Touch many lives. In fact, one person can make all of the difference. They can change the world for the better, or the worse. We have seen it many times. No, you are a force for good in this world. And you will make a great many changes. I look forward to seeing it all," the commissioner said warmly and held out a hand in friendship.

Lady Sarah accepted the hand and was glad that she had met the man, despite the circumstances.

Chapter
25

The journey back to Stickleback Hollow was a quiet one. Except for Cooky.

Cooky was hysterics that they had stayed far longer than intended, and that she would not be able to prepare all that was needed for Miss Beaumont and Mr Claydon's wedding.

The Baker boys, Cooky and Bosworth all went ahead in the smaller coach in order to reach the house as soon as possible, and put an end to Cooky's clucking.

The brigadier had hired an additional carriage to carry Richard, Alex and Oliver back home in comfort, rather than forcing them to sit in the carriage seats. Though they had made a great deal of progress and had healed well, they were not entirely health, and the carriage ride back would be uncomfortable for all of them without special arrangements being made.

Lady Sarah had not spoken two words when she had climbed into the carriage that morning. She had been lost in thought. Her mind was consumed everything that the commissioner had said to her, and the events of days before they had stopped this circle of traffickers. She knew that there would be more to come, and more lives would be ruined. All for the pursuit of money.

She tried to talk to herself, tell herself to try not to dwell too much on the fact that they had merely temporarily stopped the symptom, as it was too easy to follow that thought through to the conclusion that all of her mystery solving was merely a delaying action.

When the party returned to Stickleback Hollow, Mrs Bosworth was overjoyed to see them. And Bosworth related to the household, in full, all that had happened in Brighton, causing Mrs Bosworth to declare that never again should the group be allowed to leave the household without her.

Believing that she in some way could have prevented all the ills that had happened to them.

Lady Sarah had smiled and laughed, and been quite relieved to be back at Grangeback. The village was still a hive of activity with wedding preparations, which provided a great distraction from her dark thoughts on the trip back from Brighton.

When the big day finally dawned, the village had never looked better. Miss Beaumont's gown was an elegant one. Not overly ostentatious, but far more than she had ever expected to wear in her lifetime.

Mr Claydon looked dapper in his new suit. The pair had been so overjoyed to finally be married, that the feast given at Grangeback was one that had lasted for almost two days. It felt good to celebrate again.

Mr Hunter had been keen to attend the wedding as one of the ushers, and had been given the honour of escorting Lady Sarah to the church, much to the chagrin of Mr Brown. Lady Sarah had not spoken much to either of the two men since their capture, the guilt over their torture and injuries had meant that she had avoided them both.

"You do not need to feel guilt over what happened. I would die a thousand deaths if it would make you happy, help you in any way. To live through such a trifle as torture is nothing," Mr Hunter had whispered to her as she took his arm. She had looked at him with shock at such a statement, but still could not bring herself to forgive putting the men in danger.

The last time the village had all assembled in this

manner had been for the funeral of Grace, and now they were celebrating a wedding, the beginning of two lives now made one. Of two people were very dear to Lady Sarah.

Though she knew in the back of her mind, that there would be a great many evils that was before each and every person attendance at the wedding, at least for now, on this one day, there was joy, there was peace, and most of all, they were all together.

Love the book? Need to know what's next in Stickleback Hollow?

In the realm of peerage and privilege, mistakes can mean social death. Reputations can recover, but when the game of power turns deadly, can she find a killer before it's too late?

<u>Get At the Court of St. James now!</u>

Want to stay up-to-date on the latest news from my books? Want to get access to pre-order discounts and the chance to be part of my Advanced Reader and Street Teams? Then sign up for my newsletter here!

Looking for more than just books? You can get the latest releases from me, signed paperbacks and hardbacks, mugs, tshirts, journals and much more from my Read Round the Clock Shopify store.

Love the Mysteries of Stickleback Hollow? Not caught up with the rest of the series, then jump back to *A Thief in Stickleback Hollow*, Book 1 in the Mysteries of Stickleback Hollow and see how it all began.

Want to help a reader out? Reviews are crucial when it comes to helping readers choose their next book and you can help them by leaving just a few sentences about this book as a review. It doesn't have to be anything fancy, just what you liked about the book and who you think might like to read it.

Scan the QR Code below or visit

https://mybook.to/DayTriptoBrighton

If you don't have time to leave a review or don't feel confident writing one, recommending a book to your family, friends and co-workers can help them choose their next book, so feel free to spread the word.

Historical Note

It is widely believed that women wore woollen bathing suits when taking the waters at Brighton, even in the bathing huts that offered them privacy from prying eyes, but the truth is that the majority of women in both the Georgian and the Victorian ages swam naked in the water.

The beaches were indeed segregated due to bathing suits no existing when sea bathing was first popularised in the Georgian period and propriety mandated that men and women should not be nakedly swimming together.

The contraptions that were used for sea bathing were used exclusively by women, and were pulled out into the waves by horses or strong men. When the women wanted to come back to the shore, a flag was raised and the men or horses would go out to tow the bathing contraptions back to shore.

Women would change inside the bathing contraptions and

then diving into the water or being pushed by a burly woman that was hired to do so.

Bathing in sea water and even drinking it was considered to be extremely good for the health, and though there is some good that can come from sea bathing, it was nowhere near what the Georgians and Victorians imagined it to be. The health benefits of sea bathing including:

i.   helping to clear up skin breakouts such as acne, psoriasis and lupus. They will not cure the underlying conditions, but the symptoms can be reduced by sea bathing.

ii. heals skin abrasions due to the high salt content, it can help reduce infections and in some cases speed up the healing over of the skin.

iii. reduces anxiety and helps to improve the quality of sleep swimmers have due to the levels of magnesium in the water. A study was conducted by the National Trust which found that sea side walkers had a better quality and 47 minutes longer sleep than those who walked inland.

iv. can help to boost your immune system when

swimming in cold water. Studies have shown that swimming in cold water helps to boost your white blood cells, causing your immune system to function more effectively.

Commissioner Jonnes Smith is of my own creation, though Captain Jonnes Smith was the Chief Constable of Cheshire, I have no evidence that he had a brother, or that he was a member of the Salvation Army, if he did indeed exist. It was common practice within well-born families to have an heir to inherit money and title and the other sons would be sent into the army or the church as their professions. Captain Jonnes Smith served in the army before being Chief Constable of Cheshire, for him to have a brother in the church, and a third older brother to inherit made sense to have within the framework of social expectations of the time.

The tragedy of Commissioner Jonnes Smith and a lot of those who have worked tirelessly for organisations to put an end to injustice, disgusting practices, and to be a positive force in the world is that most will never live to see the effects their actions have. They will never know if they have succeeded or failed. For Commissioner Jonnes Smith we can only hope that the future ahead of us now will bring an end to children being endangered and trafficked, as well as abuse and paedophilia, but the reality is that is still exists and it is up to every one of us to be vigilant and look for signs that tell us children in our lives are in danger.

Luck is something that is ingrained in Western Society and we often use expressions such as "Good Luck!" "How lucky are you!" "I've always been lucky" but did you know that luck is actually an Old Norse belief? Hamingja is Old Norse for luck and it meant one of two things. Firstly it could be the personification of the concept of luck or the good fortune that an individual or family experienced. Secondly it referred to the altered appearance of shape-shifters. Obviously only one of those definitions has endured. But luck in the Old Norse belief system was not an explanation for a coincidence or something good happening by chance, but rather it was an inherited trait. If someone was particularly skilled at fishing, they would be said to have fishingluck. Kings were thought to be born with great luck and could even send luck out with their men when they went out in their name.

Though luck was not something that could be found or sought after within the Old Norse belief structure, it could be lost or the effects could wane. Something we might consider now as bad luck. There are many elements from the heroic code that Old Norse warriors would live by that are still prized by society today such as courage, resourcefulness, being sharp-witted, honesty, humility, generosity, being hospitable, being respectful, loyalty and have self-control. Most of these were virtues that were adopted or shared by other religions, but luck is one thing that stands apart from all of that and despite not being integrated into other religions has remained and become part of western culture anyway.

The autopsy that Doctor Hales carries out is light on medical detail on purpose. For those of you with medical training, you will be unsurprised, that despite my husband referring to me as Doctor Woolley (and now Doctor Finlay) that I do not have any medical training and have never carried out an autopsy. There specific steps that are followed to ensure that a body is properly examined, some of which are skipped in my version of events. This is done partly because most readers do not need a blow by blow breakdown of what happens to a body being autopsied, partly that it would make for very dry reading, and partly because without medical training a lot of the terms used to describe elements of the process will make little sense. I did elect to use the medical terms for the damage that tuberculosis does to the lungs as I felt that it was necessary and could not be avoided. I also hoped that such a description would encourage people to be vaccinated against tuberculosis if they believe in vaccinations, and if they do not, to take the disease seriously and be treated as soon as possible. It is a highly infectious and dangerous disease that should not be ignored or underestimated.

One guinea adjusted for inflation is worth about £136 today. I chose a guinea because a weeks wages in 1840 would have roughly worked out at anywhere from 3 Shillings and 9 d to 20 shillings depending on the profession. A fisherman could earn up to £60 a week in modern money for a 10 hour, six day working week. To be given £136 for the answer to one question was more than two weeks worth of work for a few minutes of conversation. I am a great believer in the value of knowledge and that those sharing hard-earned knowledge should be compensated accordingly.

The Limehouse community was the first Chinese community in London, and existed from as early as 1780. It is the district that Sherlock Holmes came shopping for opium in Sir Arthur Conan Doyle's books. It was known for its tea shops and for its opium dens. It began when Chinese sailors who had been discharged from their duties with the East India Company needed somewhere to settle. By the 1880s (40 years after this book) another community had begun to grow up around Pennyfields Lane, and a number of retired sailors began laundry services as well as restaurants. The Pennyfields Lane community consisted of settles from Shanghai, whereas the Limehouse community consisted of Cantonese sailors.

Brown's Hotel opened it's doors in 1837 and is the oldest hotel in London, and it still exists today. It is the site of the first telephone call in London, made by Alexander Graham Bell. The hotel has hosted many famous writers including JM Barrie, Oscar Wilde, Arthur Conan Doyle, Bram Stoker, and Robert Louis Stevenson. It consists of 117 rooms and was originally opened by James and Sarah Brown, the former maid and valet to Lord and Lady Byron. In 1859, the Ford Family took over the hotel and opened the first public dining room in the city. In 1889, they bought St George's Hotel that had opened next door and combined the two into the hotel we know today.

About the Author

I was born in Macclesfield, Cheshire, UK, and raised in the nearby town of Wilmslow. From an early age, I discovered I had a flair and passion for writing.

I began writing at the age of 7 and was first published in 2010. I currently live with my partner, Matt, and our two cats in Christchurch, New Zealand.

As an avid horsewoman and gamer, I also have a passion for singing, dancing, the theatre, and my garden.

Facebook: https://www.facebook.com/AuthorC.S.Woolley

Instagram: https://www.instagram.com/thecswoolley

Website: http://.mightierthanthesworduk.com

Acknowledgements

Writing can be an extremely lonely profession at times, but thankfully I never have to go through any of the pressures alone. My wonderful Matthew has been a source of constant support to me during all of my writing endeavours since we first met. I couldn't ask for a more fitting partner to share my life or love with.

Writing is not something I stumbled into either, my mother, Helen, took me, and my sisters, to the library every weekend when we were young to get different books, and I always maxed out the number of books I could get. Not only did she encourage me to read, but to write as well. To say I have been writing stories and poetry since I was 7 is not an exaggeration and the development of my writing career is due in no small part to her.

My mother-in-law, Lesley, has also been a source of unflinching and unwavering support, something I could not do without.

To Laura and Sam, who have read and offered opinions, death threats and encouragement on my early drafts, you are true treasures. Amy, you too are worth your weight and more in gold for all your love and support.

It may seem that writers only function alone, but I am blessed to be part of an amazing community of authors whom I know who have helped push me to even greater heights and success. For the last few months I have relied on a small group of friends more than most, my dearest Victoria Tait, Glenn Salter, Jacqui Penn, Theresa Papa, Michelle Nelson-Schmidt, and Chez Churton, my dear friends, thank you.

And finally, to you, dear reader, without you there would be no books, no series, no career. I want to thank you for all the time that you spend reading my work, reviewing it, and sharing it with your friends and family. Without you, there would be nothing. Thank you from the bottom of my heart.

Until we meet again in my next book, thank you and adieu.